CORDELIA CODD

CORDELIA CODD

NOT JUST THE BLUES

CLAIRE O'BRIEN

ORCHARD

ORCHARD BOOKS
338 Euston Road, London NW1 3BH
Orchard Books Australia
Level 17/207 Kent Street, Sydney, NSW 2000

First published in the UK in 2012 by Orchard Books

ISBN 978 1 40831 401 2

Text © Claire O'Brien 2012
Illustrations © David Roberts 2012

A CIP catalogue record for this book is available from the British
Library.

1 3 5 7 9 10 8 6 4 2

Printed in Great Britain

Orchard Books is a division of Hachette Children's Books,

To Ewan and Robert

1

I hate the school bus.

I'm glaring over my shoulder at the boy standing behind me. I growl at him. 'Your elbow is JABBING me in the BACK. Can you move it, PLEASE?'

He isn't budging so I shove his arm and he pulls a stupid face at me that looks like stretchy pizza cheese, and says, 'Oooh! Sorr…eeee. Temper.'

He's a lot bigger than me, but **I DON'T CARE**. I've been in a **MASSIVE GRUMP** for months. I'm a TOTAL GRUMPSTER. It's already June, the last term of Year Seven, and so far at Beckmere School I've managed to lose ALL my friends (although I've made one new one), fall behind with ALL my work and get the highest number of detentions in my registration group.

It's been an **ELEPHANT DUMP** of a year.

I'm trying to catch up with the homework so I don't end the summer term on a TOTALLY disastrous note, but I'm not optimistic. Miss Haliborn, my group tutor, says she's 'making allowances for my home circumstances'. Yeah? Then how come she wrote **persistently awkward and aggressive** in my journal today?

She's CLUELESS about my 'home circumstances'.

And before I even GET home I have to survive the journey. There's never a free seat on the bus, so loads of us end up standing. It's probably illegal to wedge us in like this. It smells bad, too, like Noah's Ark on a hot day, and the windows are thick with steam from people shouting. All the oxygen has been gobbled up and the big kids at the back are throwing leftover sandwich crusts around. The rest of us are choking on sweaty-sports-kit whiffs and wet-blazer pongs. My nose catches wafts of cloggy hair gel, chewing gum, fartiness and, to top it all, David French is munching smelly crisps with his mouth open RIGHT IN MY FACE, as if I'm not here. I can't avoid seeing the cheese and onion debris sloshing around in his big gob. There's loads of it stuck between his millions of wonky teeth. A

TRULY stomach-churning sight.

My stop is coming up, thank goodness. I can only see this because I'm far too tall for a twelve-year-old. I'm pushing my way through to the door, stepping on people's feet because I'm in a hurry. I don't mean to tread on them, but am I, Cordelia Codd, the only one screaming in my head **'GET ME OFF THIS STENCHWAGGON!!'**?

The bus jolts to a standstill. There's a hiss and swoosh as the doors scrape open. Rain-filled air rushes at me. RELIEF. I jump off. The usual insults are thrown at my back.

'Oi! Coddy! Fish fingers for dinner, is it?'

'Swimming the rest of the way, are you, Coddy?'

I ignore them. It's not their fault that they've got frogspawn for brains.

I'd like to ride my bike to school but the chances of still having two wheels and a saddle by the end of the day are pretty slim at Beckmere, so I have to catch the bus. One day I'll take taxis everywhere. One day, when I'm **the *⁺* GREATEST ⁺*⁺ costume designer in the history of cinema**.

One day.

Meanwhile, it's only a short walk from the bus

stop to my front door. I live on an estate of about fifty houses that all look the same. They were built in a hurry so some of them, especially mine, are already starting to look scruffy. The paint is peeling off the white front door and the garden is overgrown. It didn't used to be a mess but I can't take care of Mum AND the house AND the garden, even if it is only the size of a tea towel.

Most people who live around here work at the call centre in town.

'Hello, my name is Cordelia. How may I help you?'
AAAAGH!

I will NEVER work in a call centre, except maybe in the holidays, when I'm at art school, learning to design costumes.

Before she got poorly my mum used to say that I had 'vision'. She meant that I know exactly what I want to do when I'm older. She said I should hang on to my vision no matter what and keep working towards it. I'm sure she still thinks that, but she's not very talkative these days so I have to remember to remind myself. I've written it on a piece of bright yellow card in black felt tip and stuck it on the wall opposite my bed so that I see it every morning when I wake up. It's just above my pictures of

Rita Hayworth and Audrey Hepburn (two of my favourite film stars). It says:

You are going to be the greatest costume designer in the history of cinema!

Some days, watching old films is all that stops me from drowning myself in a bucket of mud. Mum and Dad have a MASSIVE collection. It covers one wall of our living room, but I still borrow films from the library or get them as presents. When Mum was well enough to go to the supermarket I used to tag along and rummage in the bargain baskets. I got some good films there: *The King and I, Gigi, An American in Paris*, and some modern films with great costumes, too, like *Titanic, Star Wars – The Phantom Menace* and *Shakespeare in Love*. But Mum doesn't go out of the house much these days so now I don't get the chance to find supermarket bargains.

I watch films over and over again so that I can draw the costumes in my sketchbook. I draw the long evening dresses and big swirly skirts and the men's suits that fit so perfectly. *An American in Paris* is mostly dancing. Gene Kelly is one of the stars in it and he was a FANTASTIC dancer. Sadly, not many boys dance like that these days – not at Beckmere School, anyway. There's no Gene Kelly or even a Billy Elliot at Beckmere. If there were I'd probably fall in love with him, even if he was shorter than me, which is quite likely as I'm the tallest girl in Year Seven, even in my flattest-flatty-flat-flat shoes. Mum says I'll be 'statuesque' one day. I looked 'statuesque' up in the dictionary and it means 'attractively tall, graceful and dignified', which sounds OK to me. It sounds like Ingrid Bergman in *Casablanca* or Katharine Hepburn in *The Philadelphia Story* (you have GOT to see those films).

Nearly home. It's at this corner, by the newsagent's and the broken payphone, that I usually start to wonder what sort of mind-weirdness Mum will be displaying tonight. By that I mean will she be in an UP mood or the usual DOWNER? I never know until I open the door.

It's been like this for weeks. If I were a teacher I'd probably say that, like me, Mum has 'behavioural problems'. Hardly surprising considering the stuff that's happened to us this year.

My life used to be quite normal. It was full of ordinary girl things – jokes, boys, music, clothes, magazines. Nowadays, I haven't got time to spend the whole of Saturday trying clothes on in the shops with Jen and Angela (my EX-best friends) or taking hours to paint each other's nails, or curl and straighten our hair.

These days I have to make sure Mum has clean clothes and gets out of bed once in a while, and takes a shower. I have to wash my school blouses and clean the loo and wipe the kitchen floor when it gets sticky. I have to check that we have enough bread and milk and whether anything has gone mouldy in the fridge. I know which day of the week it is by the jobs that need doing.

Wednesday is rubbish day. Early in the morning a huge van rattles its way around the estate to empty all the dustbins. I always hear it coming. It's my signal to rush downstairs in my pyjamas, pull the big black bag out of the kitchen bin and take it outside. When I'm rich and successful, Wednesday will be manicure, pedicure and hair day, not BIN BAG day.

Fridays are for cat litter. Mr Belly, our ginger tom, MUST have his tray emptied by then.

If I haven't done it I'll know by the terrible pong that it's at least Saturday. I can count how many days have gone by since the last time I cleaned it out by the number of poos sitting there. However, I do NOT intend to spend my life counting cat plop. One day I'll have a RIDICULOUS looking, floppy little dog with sticky-up hair, and someone else will clean the 'business' end of it. Perhaps they'll even invent a dog that doesn't poo by then.

You can spot Sundays a mile off. Everything is shut and all you can hear are church bells and lawn mowers. The whole estate is like a graveyard and my heart sinks from the unbearable DULLNESS of it. When I live in a big city nothing will EVER close. There will always be restaurants and shops to go to and parks full of people with ridiculous looking, floppy dogs like mine. We dog walkers will talk to each other about films we've seen and parties and art galleries and dresses.

Mondays are easy to remember, too. *Mondays are last-tin-in-the-cupboard days.* I have to remind Mum to go to the post office for her sickness benefit. She leaves the money on the table so that I can buy food from the corner shop when I get home. We're really skint now that Mum can't work, so I have to get what I can with her benefit money. In my glamorous future there'll be tons of exciting food in the cupboards every day and my kitchen will always smell of mouth-watering goodies.

Meanwhile, THAT'S how interesting my life is: bins, cat poo and shopping for tinned food. Some days I try to cook something, not that Mum ever eats much. It's usually

beans **on toast**

or cheese **on toast**

or tomatoes **on toast**

or pasta…maybe…sometimes, if Mum supervises me.

I'm not a good cook, not like Dad. That's his job. He's a chef. And you might wonder why he isn't doing all the cleaning and cooking and looking after Mum while she's poorly. Well, he's the REASON she's poorly, that's why. This is all HIS fault, him and the HORRIBLE man Mum used to work for, Mr Snaul.

Sometimes I'm angry with Mum for not being able to work. She doesn't even get out of bed some days. I know she can't help it so I let myself be angry with Dad instead. But he's not here for me to shout at and the FURIOUS RED FEELINGS I get have to burst out somewhere. That's why school has gone hopeless and messed-up and why I fell out with Jen and Angela, and just about everyone else in the whole FUDGE-SQUITTING world. And that's why Miss Haliborn wrote **persistently awkward and aggressive** in my journal today.

As soon as I open the front door I can tell by the smell from the rubbish bin that it hasn't been one of Mum's ^{UP} days. On her ^{UP} days Mum cleans like a whirlwind then collapses in an exhausted heap on the sofa. She doesn't have many ^{UP} days. If it had been an ^{UP} day, I'd be choking on bleach and furniture polish fumes by the time I'd kicked off my shoes.

Today is only Monday, but the bin is already overflowing. The washing-up from yesterday is piled high around the kitchen sink and Mum hasn't made it to the post office because there's no money on the table. Half a loaf of bread has been left out of the bread bin and the jam jar is standing next to it with the lid off, dribbling red stickiness. There's a fly licking itself on the rim. I shoo it away and screw the lid down.

Mr Belly has forced his way into a box of Cat Crunch. He's chewed a corner of the packet off and it looks like he's spent the whole day shoving his paw in through the hole and dragging biscuits out. There are cat snacks ALL OVER the floor.

I know Mum will be asleep on the sofa, so I just peek into the living room without calling to her. She's there, breathing deeply, her pink fleece blanket rising and falling gently. The room is stuffy and dark. Daylight peeps in through the worn-out patch near the top of the closed curtains. I go back to the kitchen and talk to Mr Belly instead. He offers me his chin so I scratch underneath it, making him purr. Then I look in the fridge and cupboards for something to cook later. All that's left is a tin of macaroni cheese.

On Mondays and Fridays, before I leave for school, I always put some washing in the machine. I empty the clean clothes out now, giving them a shake to straighten the crumples, and hang them on the big airer near the back door. Next, I write a list of jobs Mum needs to do tomorrow. My lists help her to remember what needs doing. Her memory is like a tea strainer these days – nothing stays in her head. But I know I mustn't make the job list too long or she'll have one of her STRESSY PANICS.

Mum used to do a zillion things a minute, now it's

...one

  ...thing

    ...at

      ...a

        ...time,

          ...very

            ...slowly.

Poor Mum.
I work out a list.

1. wash up
2. gather paper for recycling

I look up at the souvenir calendar we brought back from our holiday in Scotland last year. There's something written on it for tomorrow. I thought so…

3. *doctor's appointment 2.30 p.m.*
4. *read three pages of your book*

I don't know which novel Mum's reading at the moment. She used to have five or six on the go at once, piled up by her bed or near the sofa. Nowadays it's amazing if she finishes one book in a month. She says she can't concentrate any more.

By nine o'clock tonight Mum will have gone back to bed. If I'm lucky she'll get off the sofa and stay awake long enough for a bit of macaroni cheese and some toast.

I always take her a cup of tea in the morning and reset the alarm clock if she has to get up for something, like her doctor's appointment tomorrow. The tea is usually still there, cold and scummy, when I get home. Her tea used to go cold before, when she was working at the office for creepy Mr Snaul, but that was because she was always in a hurry to get moving and do fifty things before her first meeting. That's all stopped now. She filled up with sadness and worry because of what Dad did, and because Mr Snaul made her work far too hard.

She got worn out with unhappiness and having too many things to do.

'She just needs a nice long rest,' Dr Khan says.

But I think she has a br♥ken heart.

2

Back in October, when I'd just started at this school, Dad went to a big meeting down in London. It was a conference for chefs. He went to these meetings quite often, but this time he was late back. Not just a bit late, like a few hours, so that his dinner was cold and soggy, but DAYS late. Mum told me that he'd got held up by 'one thing and another'. Later, she said it was the weather.

'But the sun's shining,' I said.

She snapped back at me, 'Not down in London, it's not.'

It isn't like Mum to snap. Usually, she's really gentle.

Her handbag was on the kitchen table in front of her. She often sat there to read or think or sort out bits of paper, like bills and letters. When she snapped at me she blushed and shuffled things about in her handbag, staring into it, as if she didn't want to look at me. Much later on, I asked again, 'Any news from Dad?'

Mum was still at the kitchen table. She was picking at her fingernails and scanning the newspaper. She didn't look up but just flipped another page of the paper over and pretended to be interested in what was there.

'A friend of his needs some help,' she said. 'He's had to stay on and lend a hand.'

'What with?'

I could see that she'd opened the football pages of the paper. Mum NEVER looked at those pages. She thought football was the most boring game in the universe. So I knew she wasn't really reading the paper.

'I'm not sure,' she said. 'Something to do with work.'

'Which friend is it?' I asked.

Mum stood up quickly then, and busied herself. 'Janet. I think her name's Janet.'

She started moving packets around in the cupboards for no reason. Her hands were shaking, which got me worried. I went on at her a bit, but I needed to know what was happening.

'Will he be back tomorrow?' I asked.

Mum kept shuffling things around. 'I hope so. Now, off to school with you.'

That's when I started to feel frightened. Something must be wrong with her.

'I got BACK from school ages ago, Mum,' I said. 'It's nearly seven o'clock in the evening!'

Mum looked up at the clock. She blinked, looked down at the packets she'd taken out and spread along the worktop, then looked back at the clock. She sighed and smiled like she was trying to be cheerful, but I think she was a bit shocked at how muddled she'd got. She touched her forehead and looked like she didn't know what day it was or even what planet she was on and said, 'Goodness. What was I thinking?'

It scared me to see her all shaky and mixed up with her hands trembling over the packets of food.

'Are you all right, Mum?'

She took a deep breath and smiled again, looking at me.

'Yes, of course. I'll put some dinner on.' She stroked my hair saying, 'Don't worry, I'm just a bit tired. Dinner won't be long. Shall we have bacon and eggs? An all-day breakfast, eh?'

'Great. Yes, please.'

I didn't know what else to say so I went upstairs and put on *Breakfast at Tiffany's*. That's probably my ABSOLUTE favourite film. It's guaranteed to take my mind off ANYTHING. While I watched I tried to draw the costumes really quickly. Mr Gruber, my art teacher, says this is a good way to improve my sketching. He says it will train my eyes to spot things and my fingers to move fast. But sometimes I pause the film I'm watching so that I can add in little details from a dress or the feathers on a hat or the clip on a handbag.

My drawings were rubbish that night. I was trying to sketch the black dress that Audrey Hepburn wears right at the beginning of the film, but I couldn't concentrate. Underneath the picture I'd started, I'd drawn around my hand, like they teach you to do when you're a baby – in and out between my fingers with a pencil. I'd made the lines wobbly on purpose. It looked like Mum's hands when I saw them shaking.

We didn't talk a lot at dinner time. It was pasta and tomatoes followed by strawberry yoghurt. I don't know what happened to the all-day breakfast Mum had promised. I didn't ask. I think she'd already forgotten that she'd suggested it. Mum just

nibbled at her dinner and stared out of the window, sighing. After I'd helped clear the table I went back upstairs to finish watching *Breakfast at Tiffany's*.

Long after I'd switched off the film and got into bed, I was still lying awake. Through the dark I heard whispering. Maybe I listened for an hour, maybe it was only ten minutes, I don't remember – time goes a bit weird when you're lying in the dark. The whispering continued and I knew I'd NEVER get to sleep until I found out what was going on, so I crept downstairs, planning to pretend that I'd come to get a glass of milk.

Mum was just hanging up the phone. She was still sitting at the kitchen table – exactly where I'd left her hours ago. At first she didn't see me standing by the door. She didn't know I was there when she burst into tears and put her head on the table. The surface hadn't been wiped and strands of her lovely long brown hair spread out into the crumbs and drips of coffee. It was silent crying. Her shoulders were moving up and down. I hadn't seen a grown-up sobbing before, except in films, where they do it all the time. It's VERY different when it's real, when it's your own mum all out of control and soggy with her nose running like a baby's. It's PROPERLY frightening. But if I knew what the problem was, perhaps it wouldn't seem so scary? I spoke very quietly.

'Mum?'

She jumped and sat up, surprised to see me downstairs so late, then wiped her face on a piece of kitchen roll that was screwed up in her hand, sniffed and gave me a wonky smile, like she couldn't quite hold it straight because she was so upset and wanted to sob again.

'Oh, dear. Oh, Coco. Sit down, love.'

Only Mum and Dad call me Coco.

'What's wrong? What's happened, Mum?'

She patted the table opposite her. My chair was pulled out and I didn't move it in. I didn't want to get too close because she looked terrible, so different from how she usually looked, pretty and smiling. I was a bit scared of her because I'd never seen her like this before but then I felt guilty that I didn't want to cuddle her, even though she was so upset.

I think I already knew what she was going to tell me but I didn't want it to be happening. It was like when you fall down some stairs or out of a tree, or onto a hard pavement. You've already started to lose your balance but you can't get it back and you know there's a terrible pain flying towards you, about to smash into you.

You can't stop it.

You can't control what's coming.

A HORRIBLE moment. The moment everything changes.

'I'm sorry, Coco,' she said, 'but I don't think Dad wants to come home.'

'What d'you mean?' I asked, screwing my face up. 'Why would he NOT want to come home? Everyone wants to come home.'

Mum's bottom lip went wobbly and her eyes, which were already a mass of mascara blotches and redness, filled up with tears again.

'Dad and I have had a long talk and he's told me that he's met another lady he wants to be with more than me. He wants to stay in London.'

I felt sick. A hot feeling shot up behind my eyes

and ears and along my fingers so I had to squeeze my fists tight to stop them exploding. My face didn't move for a moment, then I leaned forward and shouted at Mum, like it was her fault.

'Then he's STUPID and *I HATE HIM*.'

And I ran upstairs, leaving Mum alone in the kitchen.

Why would he want to leave us? How could he love someone more than Mum, who was beautiful and never got cross with him even though he was always late for things and was the most untidy person on the planet? And why would he leave ME? We cooked things together and had fun and went on holidays. Had he secretly *HATED* doing all those things and not told us?

I didn't cry.

I tore up my best sketch of the black dress from *Breakfast at Tiffany's*. I ripped it into a million tiny pieces. Then I threw myself on the bed and thumped my pillow over and over and OVER until I fell asleep.

That all happened back in October, right at the start of Year Seven, my first year at Beckmere. Two and a half terms have gone by since then. Christmas and my birthday have already passed. The weather might have got better, but LIFE has got MUCH worse since Dad did his disappearing act.

I've only once said out loud that I miss him, but I feel it ALL the time.

Mum tried extra hard to keep things normal. She tried TOO hard really, doing lots of stuff like taking me to the cinema and to the big shopping mall by the motorway. I think she wanted to take my mind off it all, but every time she took me somewhere I couldn't help thinking how much better it would've been if Dad was there with us. Of course, I didn't say that to her. All I said was, 'I miss Dad.'

I only said it once, when we had baked beans for the third night running.

Dad cooked fresh, spicy food. Everything had flavour and ZING. Now my WHOLE life felt like dry, white toast with nothing more interesting on it than baked beans.

All Mum said was, 'I know, love. I miss him, too.'

3

I suddenly had a **50%** reduction in parents and
no say in the matter. I was angry all the time and it
wouldn't stay inside me. By the Christmas holidays
I'd managed to fall out with my best friends, Jen
and Angela. I didn't mean it to happen, but I'd
started flying into BAZOOKA tempers with people
who never used to annoy me at all. Mum was still
working at the office then and I already had to
help out lots more than before with things at home
because Dad wasn't there to do his share. It was OK
for Jen and Angela; they only had to think about
their usual worries:

* How will I get this homework done?

* Do my friends like my new hair slides?

* Has boy X noticed me yet?

* Shall I go to Netball or Drama Club, or both?

* Will I get to see that new film everyone's talking about?

* Will I be allowed to go to X's party on Friday?

I had all those things to stress about PLUS SO MUCH MORE. Now that Dad was gone, I had a HUGE extra brain-ache beyond the usual torments of Year Seven, and an empty, scared feeling most of the time. Really, I didn't care a **RAT'S EYEBALL** any more about homework and boys and hair slides and Netball and Drama. I COULDN'T care about those things because there just wasn't room in my head along with worrying about Dad and about all the jobs that needed doing at home.

When you aren't COMPLETELY obsessed

with the usual girl stuff there's not much else left to talk about with friends like Jen and Angela.

And I got especially mean and snappy if anyone mentioned dads, which OF COURSE they did, LOADS.

My dad drives me nuts.
My dad's got a new car.
My dad grounded me AGAIN.
My dad's taking me skiing.
My dad's an old hippy.
My dad sulks in the shed.
Mydadthis, mydadthat.
Dad, *Dad,* DAD.

The 'D' word was everywhere.

One morning, a few weeks before Christmas, when Jen and Angela were talking about stuff they were going to do with their families in the holiday and I didn't have ANY plans and not much of a family left, I really lost it.

Jen and Angela both knew that Dad wasn't around any more but they carried on talking about their own dads and their own holiday plans as if I had no feelings about half my parents vanishing. Then, after YET ANOTHER argument with HER dad, Jen came flouncing into the registration group.

Now her dad is, I admit, a COMPLETE control freak, but she went ON and ON about how mean he was. Jen was ALWAYS complaining about him, with her eyes rolling, swishing back her blonde hair. Recently, she'd started to remind me of Miss Piggy when she did this, so I told her. It was one of those things that you might think but you'd NEVER say out loud, not to someone who was your friend. But I said it, RIGHT to her face. I just **FLIPPED**.

'You look just like Miss Piggy when you flounce about, do you know that?'

Jen went VERY red and shoved her hands onto her hips, which made her look even more like Miss Piggy. I couldn't help laughing out loud at her.

She shouted, 'Oh, *thanks*, Cordelia! You're supposed to *sympathise*. You know what a *nasty* old *grinch* my dad is.'

'Yeah, but d'you have to go on about it SO much?'

I couldn't believe what I was doing. I was falling out with her BIG TIME by just being totally…well… honest and truthful about what I REALLY thought. I must've had these feelings bottled up inside for ages and now here they were, flooding out, and I couldn't stop them, even though I knew this meant CERTAIN DEATH for our friendship.

Jen SHRIEKED back at me.

'Yes, I do have to go on about it *actually*, or I'll go *mad*!'

Angela giggled nervously and looked down at her feet. She wasn't as confident as Jen and was a bit scared of arguments. She was probably wishing the bell would ring and interrupt us. But it didn't. More and more things I'd been thinking about Jen came pouring out of my mouth.

'You're spoiled rotten, y'know? Your dad buys you LOADS of stuff.'

Jen's mouth fell open. I hadn't noticed before that she already had a big filling in one of her back teeth.

'He does *not*. I don't have an expensive bike, like *you*, or ice skates, like *you*, or a fancy watch, like *you*.'

I sneered at her, really HORRIBLY, like she was the most STUPID person I'd ever met.

'They're all OLD things passed on from my mum's friends, and you KNOW that. I don't get holidays three times a year, like YOU, and riding lessons, like YOU, and new shoes practically every week, like YOU.'

Then I had a final **EXPLOSION** and shouted the most hurtful thing I could think of.

'You should realise how LUCKY you are and stop being such a FAT BRAT.'

And I stormed off.

Jen was super-sensitive about her weight so I knew I'd said the one thing GUARANTEED to upset her. I felt hot tingles behind my eyes and I ran into the toilets to cry. Falling out with Jen and Angela was like another big chunk had dropped off my life. First Dad, now them. Everything was changing. I was changing. The weird thing about it was that I think I WANTED to break away from Jen and Angela, I just hadn't meant to be horrible about it and I didn't think it would happen yet, not for ages. I was suddenly a different person and I didn't fit in with them like I used to. I wished that I did but there was no going back. The scariest thing was that I didn't seem to fit ANYWHERE any more. I felt like a firework bouncing off the walls, not knowing where I'd land or when all the fizzing and banging in my head would stop.

Jen and Angela haven't spoken to me since, except to say bitchy things. They've both CUT ME OUT. I don't exist any more as far as they're concerned. Jen sent me a text the afternoon of our argument. It said:

UR deleted 4EVER frm my fone.

Everyone else in our crowd soon did the same: Bella Hassington, Craig Downey, Farah Shah. They all looked STRAIGHT through me and never texted or called after that. I'm not surprised. If I were them, I'd probably hate me, too.

Jen was the popular one, I'd always been in her shadow, so when we fell out she still had a cosy group of mates around her and I was left out in the cold.

She isn't THAT pretty, but she has loads of confidence and a big smile that will never need a brace, and golden hair that makes boys look when she walks down the corridor. Mine is brown and straight. Not shiny, shampoo-advert sort of straight, just boring. I used to curl it, or straighten it even more and brush it loads, but I don't have time now. A quick comb in the morning and that's it. I shove it into an elastic band so that it doesn't get in the way. If I don't tie it back it falls into Mr Belly's dish when I'm feeding him, or into the washing-up bubbles, or into the dustpan when I'm sweeping up mess in the kitchen.

After the argument, at first I wanted to say 'sorry' and make up with Jen and Angela before everyone disappeared for the Christmas holiday, but I was scared that Jen might just tell me to get lost in front of loads of other kids, so I didn't dare.

Instead, on dry days, when we were allowed onto the playing fields, I started to take my sandwiches (made by me) and walk as far away from the school buildings and people as I could get, right up to the wire fence at the bottom of the sports field where cars heading for the motorway rush by. There was a pile of old milk crates there that made a good bench. Sometimes I sat on them for the whole lunch break, even when it was so cold that my fingers turned blue. I thought about Dad, wondering where he was and what he was doing.

WHY would he leave me behind? Was it SO terrible having me as a daughter? Was I THAT bad? I thought you were supposed to love your children and want to be with them no matter how terrible they turned out to be, even if they became bank robbers or murderers.

I must be worse than a criminal, I decided, if my own dad didn't want to be with me. And I thought that when you fall in love it was supposed to be with one special person? Could Dad love Mum AND this other person, this Janet? I REALLY hoped that she'd turned out to be horrible and a SHOUTER who told him off all the time for leaving things lying around, and that her breath smelled like school toilets – then he'd SERIOUSLY regret not coming home.

Dad wrote to me once, back in October, when he first disappeared.

The letter was full of lines I'd heard in films. Later, I learned that these are called clichés – KLEE-SHAYS.

I argued out loud with every sentence.

Flat 8
146 Balerno Crescent
London
NW1 2ZX

20th October

My darling Coco,

Not darling enough for you to stay with me, obviously.

I miss you so much.

So why aren't you here, then?

You'll understand when you're older why I can't be with you at the moment.

*That doesn't help me right **NOW**, does it?*

I'm sure you would like my friend, Janet.

*I doubt that **VERY MUCH**. All women called Janet are the enemy...**FOR EVER**. How **DARE** you even mention her name!!*

Mum and I will soon be friends again and I will be able to visit.

*Don't visit...a visit **WILL NOT DO**. A visit means you go away again.*

I'm living in London, as you probably know. We are trying to start another café.

***WE** used to mean you and Mum.*

Meanwhile, I'm working in a restaurant that you'd hate. It's not at all glamorous, the way you like things. Everything is greasy. I would love you to come and stay with me, but I don't have a nice flat yet. Maybe soon.

That means never.

Please remember that I love you and think about you often.

*Yeah, like when? You really expect me to believe **THAT!?***

With all my love,

Are you sure your girlfriend can spare any?

DAD xxxxx

*Save your kisses for **THE EVIL JANET***

My ears made a banging sound inside when I read it. I felt red and sweaty and **FUMING**. My breathing pushed and sucked, in and out between my teeth. Then I tore up the letter, folding and tearing and ripping and SCRUNCHING the little pieces, and threw them as far under my bed as I could make them go.

4

Christmas was DOG POO ON TOAST. We'd always spent Christmas at Dad's restaurant before, ever since I was tiny. It was MAD busy with customers, and Mum and I helped out. My job was to fold the red linen napkins for the waitress to put on the tables and to polish the cutlery with a clean cloth until it sparkled. I got to pull about a MILLION crackers with the customers. It was like a big party that went on for days. But last Christmas, for the first time ever, we had hardly ANY customers. Dad said it was because of something called the RECESSION, which kind of meant that the whole world had run out of spare money, so not many people could afford to eat at nice restaurants like ours.

Remembering how busy it used to be, full of people laughing and chatting, and the smell of wine corks and brandy butter and hot puddings, and how happy Dad was when he was cooking, made this Christmas feel COMPLETELY grey and sad in comparison.

At the beginning of the holiday I kept wondering what Jen and Angela were doing. They would have gone to at least one great party and done their last-minute Christmas shopping together. I could just see them, trying on every party dress in the pre-Christmas sales. Once or twice I hoped that one of them might call. FAT CHANCE – I was so far out of the picture that I was invisible as far as they were concerned. And I didn't REALLY want to make it up with them, I was just bored and miserable.

I did my Christmas shopping with Mum, but I refused to buy a present for Dad, which Mum said would upset him.

'Why should I care? He's upset me, hasn't he?' I said. 'You don't buy presents for people who don't want to be with you.'

Mum sat down on a seat in the shopping mall. I sat next to her.

'He does want to be with you, Coco. It's just...'

'Just what? Just that he'd rather be with someone called Janet, hundreds of miles away?'

'No, it's just that he's a bit muddled up at the moment. When the restaurant stopped making money and he had to sell it, he got very tired and upset and he didn't know what to do.'

'So he ran away to London? How was that supposed to help? He could just've got another job, couldn't he?'

I could tell that Mum didn't know what else to say. She just shook her head and sighed.

'Try to be kind to him, Coco. I know he's done a stupid thing, but he's not a bad man really.'

I knew Dad couldn't SUDDENLY have changed into a total stinking loser. He must still have been OK somewhere deep down. But I wasn't ready to be kind to him and I didn't understand how Mum could be.

We got on with our shopping because neither of us wanted to argue in the middle of town and everywhere was getting so crowded that we just wanted to get home. I found a soft scarf for Mum that was gold and green and would look lovely next to her chestnut hair, and a bangle made of hundreds of little beads in the same green and gold colours. I made her go into another shop while I chose them. When she came back, Mum had some news.

'Coco, I've just had a phone call. There's a chance that Granny Twigg might be coming for Christmas. You'd better get her a little something.'

My face turned white. Christmas was never going to be much good without Dad, but now it was RUINED. It should've been a relaxing time, just Mum and me watching films together downstairs on the big television. We might have sat there all day, with her crying at the romantic bits and me drawing costumes.

But instead, a few days later, Granny Twigg arrived. She hadn't been to visit us at Christmas for a long time because she didn't like Dad. Now that he wasn't there she invited herself and IMMEDIATELY began bossing me and Mum about. Granny Twigg is Mum's mum and she is absolutely convinced that we are all 'destined to fall into the FIRES OF HELL' because we don't go to church. I think I could put up with that if she was a nice person – but she isn't. She says mean things about EVERYONE.

Granny Twigg is small and bony and wears several cardigans at the same time. Each layer of cardigan is uglier than the last. She never wears lipstick and never smiles and her hair is chopped short by a rubbish hairdresser who makes it stick out at funny angles. Her glasses swing on a chain around her neck and she has a weird smell, which Mum told me is mothballs. Apparently, mothballs will stop moths eating her ugly cardigans when she puts them away in a drawer for summer.

'Even moths wouldn't want to eat THOSE cardigans,' I said.

'Moths have no fashion sense and will eat anything woolly,' Mum replied, trying not to laugh. She also said that I MUST NOT EVER mention the mothball smell to Granny, as it would upset her.

'But she upsets US all the time,' I said.

Mum said that wasn't the point.

I'm not sure what the point IS of being nice to someone who clearly thinks you are evil and going to Hell, but I didn't go on about it because Mum had been working so hard at the office and was tired and broken-hearted, so she didn't need me having arguments about Granny smells to add to her problems.

To survive GT's (Granny Twigg's) visit I stayed in my room watching Audrey Hepburn in *Roman Holiday* and *Sabrina* over and over again. In *Roman*

Holiday she's a princess who runs away, pretends that she's an ordinary girl and has adventures. She has her long princess hair cut short and even gets into a fight. And in *Sabrina* she's a poor girl who loves a rich man who is her dad's boss, but he's not interested in her because she's too ordinary. Then she goes to Paris and comes back all glamorous and beautiful and THEN he wants to marry her, except that he's not a very nice man – so someone much better has to come along for her to fall in love with who is nice and kind. I made sketches of most of the dresses Audrey Hepburn wears in those two films. Watching them over and over at Christmas meant I got better and better at drawing costumes.

I did my best to behave well so that Mum wouldn't get an earful of nagging from GT about what a MONSTROUS child I am. I even let GT march me off to St Patrick's Church THREE TIMES. I thought it would give Mum a chance to have a lie in, and I didn't EVEN argue when she said that Mum was lazy, just because there was a bit of dust on our mantelpiece. Instead, I got a duster and wiped it myself so that she'd SHUT UP and leave Mum alone. It was like protecting my mum from a school bully. If she hadn't been an old lady,

I would have HAD to kick her. Honestly, I only managed to control my temper by reminding myself that she would clear off and go home in a few days.

Not kicking my granny this Christmas was the hardest thing I've EVER done; I should have been given a medal by the queen. Grannies are supposed to be soft and cuddly and fun, and good at baking big spongy cakes. Well, something went seriously wrong with THIS granny. This granny believes that women should do ALL the cooking. Dad used to do all the cooking in our house, which is one of the many things she didn't like about him. And, actually, I think some women, like HER, should be banned from EVER cooking ANYTHING. She fed us dumplings, and tea that was so strong I had to screw my eyes up to drink it, and white bread and soggy boiled carrots and soggy boiled potatoes and soggy boiled meat that tasted like elastic bands. While she was chopping and boiling everything to death she prattled on about how HOPELESS Mum was in the kitchen. Chop, chop, chop at the carrots, nag, nag, nag at me and Mum.

Her voice droned ON
and ON
and *ON*.

I don't think she even stopped to breathe. I REALLY had to hold myself back from WALLOPING her with a saucepan. Instead, I tried to have a reasonable conversation. I only tried this once before giving up and going back to watching films in my room.

'Dad's a brilliant cook,' I told her. 'Lots of men are great cooks. What about Jamie Oliver, Rick Stein, Gordon Ramsay, Hugh Fearnley-What's-his-name?'

Granny Twigg just sniffed. I don't think she'd heard of any celebrity chefs.

'Dad's a better cook than you,' I said, swallowing hard because I knew I'd gone too far.

I waited for the ceiling to fall in on me but Granny Twigg just lifted her chin and looked down her nose at me.

'Yes, well, he's not here, is he?' she said.

The words pushed out of her tight, wrinkly mouth like poisonous worms. She enjoyed saying it. She enjoyed saying hurtful things.

I don't know why I was sticking up for Dad, though. He deserved a good kick, too. And I was cross with Mum for not standing up to GT. Dad would have. He didn't take any nonsense from her. That's probably why she was being so nasty about him now, because he wasn't there to give her an argument. Mum just let her get on with her moaning. It was like Mum had a special button she pressed that made her stop hearing the CONSTANT nagging, like the mute button on the TV control.

Dad and I used to pull faces when Granny Twigg was rattling on, trying to make each other burst into giggles. Everything she said was something MEAN AND SCRATCHY about someone else. Dad said (when GT couldn't hear) that if she stopped finding things wrong with people, she would run out of things to say. It was the only way she knew how to talk.

On Christmas morning I thought I'd wear something INTERESTING so I came downstairs in my stripy tights, a little green skirt and a big, black shirt. I had a lovely belt and some dangly earrings that Mum had bought for me in the sales. I thought it all went together really well, but GT took one look at me, sniffed and said that I was just like her sister, who she called 'That *La-Di-Dah* Deirdre'.

Now, I only met Great-auntie Deirdre a couple of times before she died last year and I thought she was great fun. She was Granny Twigg's sister, but they were TOTALLY different. Deirdre always held a long cigarette holder between her fingers with a coloured cigarette in it that she never lit – I don't think she ever really smoked – and she had silver hair that was wavy and soft and very smart. She wore stockings with seams up the back and wide skirts with lots of material in them, and petticoats underneath that rustled when she walked. There was always a shiny belt around her waist and on top she wore pretty blouses with the collar turned up at the neck. She had lovely jewellery, too, and every ring and bracelet and necklace had a story that came with it. I loved hearing about where she had bought things, they were always part of an adventure she'd had in glamorous-sounding places like Milan, Como, Nice, Hong Kong or Rio de Janeiro. When I looked those places up in our big atlas it made me want to travel all over the world like she had done.

Granny Twigg said that Deirdre was too bothered about how she looked and that her stockings with seams were 'shocking' and 'frivolous'. She said Deirdre was 'showy'. When GT had a good moan about someone who had got old and died, which was quite often, she always ended with, 'You can be sure she/he is in the *hot place* now.'

GT said 'hot place' with her lips skinny and

tight, and with a nod towards the carpet. She was always warning me about the *hot place*.

Until Mum and Dad explained this to me I used to think the *hot place* meant the cellar underneath Granny Twigg's house, where the boiler bubbled away. When Auntie Deirdre died we all went to GT's house after the funeral so, while the grown-ups were eating her mean little egg sandwiches and bullet-hard cake, I crept down to the cellar, expecting to find the ghost of Auntie Deirdre there. After a while I came back up to let GT know that Auntie Deirdre wasn't in the *hot place*. I told her that there was just an old bicycle down there, a pile of coal and a trap with a dead mouse in it that smelled a bit funny.

'She's in a warmer place than that, make no mistake,' Granny Twigg told me, shaking her head.

'Like Brazil?' I asked.

She got a bit irritated by that question.

'No, child,' she said, with a straggly crumb of sandwich stuck to the corner of her mouth, 'like ETERNAL DAMNATION.'

Her eyes narrowed when she said this, in a spiteful sort of way, like it wasn't a good place to go and she was glad her sister had been sent there.

So I asked Dad where ETERNAL DAMNATION
was. It didn't sound as good as Rio de Janeiro or
Milan, or any of the places Auntie Deirdre would
WANT to go. Dad laughed out loud, right there in
the middle of the funeral tea. He laughed and then
nearly choked on a piece of the bullet-hard fruitcake
and said Eternal Damnation was the same as saying
that someone had gone to Hell because they were
bad, but that it only existed inside the heads of
people who had forgotten how to enjoy themselves,
like Granny Twigg. Then he told GT off. He said
she was filling my head with 'nonsense'.

They had a HUMDINGER of a row. I didn't
understand most of it. Mum and the other guests
were scarlet with embarrassment. GT was scarlet
with rage. The red faces of the grown-ups were
the only brightly coloured things in the whole of
Granny Twigg's house, I noticed. Everything else
was the colour of mushrooms and digestive biscuits.

We weren't invited to GT's house after that.

On the way home Dad told me that Great-
auntie Deirdre had been 'a fine old gadabout'. I
asked him what that was and he told me it was
someone who had a great time doing lots of
different things. He said that she liked interesting

people and lovely places. She was a 'character', he said, and he and Mum had loved her very much.

'If Auntie Deirdre is *anywhere* now that she's dead,' Mum added, 'I'm sure that the sun is shining and there is a great party going on.'

So it didn't bother ME when Granny Twigg said that I was like 'That ***La-Di-Dah*** Deirdre'. I was actually quite pleased. I think I'd like to be 'a fine old gadabout' when I'm wrinkly.

Poor old Granny Twigg. Dad used to say that she needed her 'happiness switch' mending. I didn't feel very sorry for her this Christmas, though. THIS Christmas Mum and I needed jolliness and great food, and for kind things to be said. GT just made everything GRIM. And, just when I thought things couldn't get any worse, she gave me JELLY BABIES and a second-hand BARBIE as a present, like I was six years old and a desperate refugee. I managed not to look horrified and said 'thank you' to her. Mum and I laughed about it later, but it was HORRIBLE at the time.

Just after we'd opened our presents in the morning, Dad rang. He had sent me two beautiful new sketchbooks and some expensive pencils and pastels as well as FIVE films for a present, so I should have rushed to thank him, but I didn't.

When the phone rang Granny Twigg was busy bossing Mum about in the kitchen again, chopping and boiling food to a pulp while she gave orders about how things should be done. Mum came out of the kitchen all red and flustered. She closed the door behind her before she answered the phone. Perhaps she knew it was going to be Dad. Sometimes people who love each other know when the other person is going to ring. I've seen it in films. The one who's answering the phone tidies their hair before they pick up the receiver and the person waiting on the other end for them to answer looks worried in case the person isn't there. Sometimes in films the screen is split into two parts so you can see both people at the same time.

When the phone rang, I was in my room, keeping away from the brussel sprout smells and GT's grouchy voice. I paused *Gilda* – a film I've watched six times, at least – and went to sit at the top of the stairs. Perhaps I knew it was Dad, too.

Mum looked like a lovely actress, a modern one. She leaned against the wall in her apron and comfy old jeans. Her hair was piled on top of her head with a clip holding it that had green sparkly

bits. It was her Christmas clip, she'd told me earlier.
I think she bought it to cheer herself up. My mum
is as beautiful as a film star, but with a slightly beaky
nose, like mine.

On the phone, Dad was doing most of the
talking. I couldn't make out what he was saying, but
I could hear the sound of his voice going up and
down like music. He spoke quite slowly at first, then
got quicker, like he was pretending to sound happy
and had interesting news. Mum didn't say much.
I could tell she was cross and wanted to shout
because she had her free hand tucked deep into her
jeans pocket and her shoulders were hunched up.
While I watched and listened I made an imaginary
dress for her. It was fiery red and long and she had
black velvet shoes with twinkly bits on them. The
dress was the colour that feeling angry would be if
you could paint it. I stayed at the top of the stairs
where she could see me because I thought that if
she knew I was listening she probably WOULDN'T
start a row with Dad. I didn't want her to shout at
Dad – I wanted to do that MYSELF.

So, when she asked if I'd like to talk to Dad I
nodded, came halfway down the stairs and took
the phone from her. His voice was extra especially

gentle. I hadn't heard it for ages and I wanted to cry.

'Hi, Coco.'

He sounded like it was hard for him to say my name, like there was something stuck in his throat.

'Hi,' he said again. 'How're you doing?'

But I just couldn't be nice to him. He didn't deserve it. I wanted my voice to sound like a punch.

'Pretty CRAP, actually. What d'you care?'

Mum frowned, but she didn't stop me or take the phone off me.

'I care a lot, Coco. You know I do,' Dad said.

'If you cared, you'd be here with me and Mum.'

'I was hoping you'd reply to my letter.'

'Why should I?'

'Coco, I know you're upset.'

'Dead right, I'm upset. I have a crap dad who hasn't even turned up for Christmas. What d'you expect?'

'Mum and I need to sort a lot of things out, Coco.'

'Why can't you sort them out HERE?'

'That's not possible just now, Coco. I wish it was. I miss you.'

'Well, that's YOUR FAULT, isn't it? You cleared off.'

'Yes, yes, you're right, love.'

Then I **SCREAMED** at him.

'I **HATE** you for doing this. Everything was all

right until **YOU DID THIS**. You should be HERE helping us get Christmas dinner ready. You're a PIG and you DON'T love us or you'd **NEVER** have gone away.'

Then I burst into tears and threw the phone downstairs. Mum caught it, put it to her ear and turned her back to me, saying gently, 'That's enough, Coco. Go back upstairs. I'll be up in a minute.'

As I flounced back to my room I heard her say down the phone to Dad, 'Do you see what you've done?'

Mum didn't get back upstairs for ages to talk to me because Granny called her into the kitchen as soon as she'd hung up. By then, I had thrown myself onto my bed and chucked my cushion collection all around the room, really hard, wishing they could smash through the walls.

On Boxing Day, Granny Twigg left. HOORAY! She got a taxi to the station before breakfast so that she could catch the only train running that day.

For one short moment I was happy.

Mum flopped down on the sofa and cried as soon as she'd gone. She smiled at the same time and said that they were 'tears of relief' that she wasn't going to have another dumpling and boiled carrot dinner. I could tell that she was just saying that to make me feel better. I knew she was crying because Granny Twigg was her mum and she was supposed to be kind to her, but she'd just made her EVEN MORE tired and upset than she was before.

We stayed quiet for the rest of the day, watching films and cuddling and enjoying the fact that no one was nagging or upsetting us. Mum and I stick to romantic films or funny films. She understands that I have to draw while I'm watching and is very patient if I have to keep stopping and skipping back to get a better look at what someone is wearing. I'm not really excited by the boy/girl kissing stuff in films, and someone is ALWAYS kissing, or thinking about kissing, or else dancing and singing. Mum likes that soppy stuff, though. She cries into a hankie while I'm scribbling away in my sketchbook.

'I don't know what all the fuss is about,' I tell her. 'It's not real.' But sometimes I don't think my mum realises this.

It was Mum and Dad who got me interested

in watching old films in the first place. They were at university together and they ran a club called a film society. Every week they were allowed to use a big room at the university and a projector and show old films to their friends. Sounds great to me! Mum told me that she once wanted to run her own cinema, a little place that showed just one film at a time, not like the big multi-screen place at the shopping mall. After we had watched *My Fair Lady* and before we started *Lemony Snicket* I remembered about her dream cinema. I asked her to describe it to me again.

'What, now?'

'Yes, I want to hear about it again,' I said.

'OK. Well, it has red velvet seats, and some of the seats are doubles, like sofas, so that people can cuddle up together if they want. There is a huge golden chandelier hanging from the ceiling and velvet curtains across the screen. A man in an evening suit plays the piano as the customers come in and there are waiters who will take your order for a glass of wine or fruit juice or a cup of tea without you having to leave your comfortable seat. Every seat has a special place to put your glass or cup, like a little table. It's the cosiest, friendliest cinema in the world.'

'Why don't you do it?' I asked.

'Well, that used to be our plan. Once Dad's restaurant was making enough money I was going to stop working at the office and open a little cinema, but then the restaurant stopped making any money at all. Things just didn't work out like we'd expected.' She sighed and looked sad. 'That's life,' she said.

'No,' I said, sitting up straight and giving her shoulder a shake. 'It absolutely is NOT. You're not old yet; you can still do it.'

But Mum just looked tired. I wanted to tell her off.

'It's just like me with my costumes. You had a "vision", didn't you?' I was frowning and looking impatient. 'It's just the same.'

'Yes, I suppose I did have a vision,' Mum admitted.

'Well then, what did you say to me? HANG ON TO YOUR VISION AND KEEP GOING, COCO. That's what you said.'

Then Mum laughed and her eyes twinkled. She looked surprised that I'd remembered what she said. AS IF I'd forget.

'So you DO listen to me sometimes, Coco Codd?'

'Of course I do, sometimes.'

Then Mum changed the subject quickly.

'Are we going to watch *Lemony Snicket* now?' she asked.

I must never be like Mum, I thought. I must never forget that I'm going to be **the ⋆⋆ GREATEST ⋆⋆ costume designer in the history of cinema**. If you let your special dream fade away you could end up sitting on the sofa feeling miserable every day.

In this house, I'll never run out of new things to watch to help with my dream. I COULD watch some of Dad's cheesy old horror films now that I'm twelve. Apparently, Dad wrote essays at university about zombie and vampire films. Whole essays! Imagine! There are films in his collection called things like *Attack of the Giant Leeches* and *I Bury the Living*. Dad and I were going to start watching these together after my twelfth birthday. He said that they're too silly to be scary and most of them are only a PG certificate. But I'm not interested in them now that he's not here. How could I watch them without him? It'd be boring and I'd keep expecting him to walk in with a bowl of his homemade popcorn. It's all HIS fault that I may never know what the costumes are like in *It Came from the Swamp* and *Monster from the Black Lagoon.*

5

I was dreading going back to Beckmere after Christmas. New Year had been peaceful. Mum didn't have to go straight back to work because the office was closed for the holidays and with Granny Twigg out of our hair there was lots of time for us to eat pizza and watch films together. BLISS. But as the first day of school got closer, I remembered that I was going back to ZERO friends. Nothing would've changed. Jen and Angela wouldn't automatically be my mates again just because it was a new year and a new term.

After break on the first morning, I was trying to get along the science corridor, pushing and shoving like everyone else so that I could get to the lab on time for Mrs Duvall's lesson. Eventually, I gave up my attempt to get through all the kids, who smelled of cold winter air and sneaky fag smoke, and ducked into the toilets to wait for the rush to pass. And I walked in on something I wasn't supposed to see.

Jen and Angela were standing in front of another girl with their backs to me. Even though I couldn't see her face I could tell straight away from her mass of frizzy hair sticking out at the sides that it was Drusilla Drummond-Steinway.

We called her **DREINSTEIN**.

A ***whiz*** kid,

genius child,

`know-all`,

smarty-pants.

Because Jen and Angela had their backs to the door they didn't see me. The first thing I noticed was that Jen had put on weight over Christmas. Her uniform trousers were getting really tight across her bum. Angela was standing right beside her, arms crossed, nodding at what Jen was saying to Drusilla. I don't think Drusilla noticed me. She was hidden by Jen.

'I want the WHOLE essay. I want YOUR essay. You can write another one.'

Drusilla didn't reply. I couldn't see if she was crying or not. Jen continued, with Angela egging her on like a nasty little goblin.

'If I don't get it by Wednesday morning, typed properly so that it's not in your handwriting, you'll find that frizzy hair of yours in piles on the floor.' She made a scissors movement with her fingers.

'Snip, Snip. Get it?'

Then I did something I'm CRINGE-MAKINGLY ashamed of. I backed out of the toilets and headed off through the crowded corridor again. I should've stuck up for Drusilla, even though she's the biggest DWEEBO in the school. I backed out because a tiny part of me still wanted to be accepted by Jen and Angela even though I could see how spiteful they were being and even though I knew we hadn't got much in common any more. If I'd stuck up for Dreinstein I'd be instantly infected with her dorkiness and called the same horrible names as her, and no one would ever let me back into their crowd. I was SUCH a chicken. I edged out into the corridor and left Drusilla to her terrible fate. When I look back now at what happened afterwards, I'm so

ASHAMED that I could bury myself in black slime and never come out again.

I knew exactly what Jen was doing. We'd been given an essay to do for English. We had to write five hundred words about a novel we'd read over the Christmas holidays, or were SUPPOSED to have read. Mr Grimpson had said that he would prefer us to choose a book from his list, which included:

- *The Curious Incident of the Dog in the Night-Time* by Mark Haddon
- *How I Live Now* by Meg Rosoff
- *Blood Pressure* by Alan Gibbons
- *I, Coriander,* by Sally Gardner

and about six or seven others that I can't remember. He said that they were books that would 'stretch' most of us. Not many of us had heard of any of them, except Drusilla, of course. She'd read most of them already. The rest of us were unlikely to have read anything other than *Harry Potter, Horrid Henry* and a few comics since we were six years old. We were supposed to go to the library and take out one of the books on the list. I'd forgotten completely until it was too late and the library was closed for Christmas, but – LUCKY ME – I found one of them in a charity shop when I went with

Mum to buy last-minute Christmas cards. I'd started reading *I, Coriander,* which is a great story, but I'm a slow reader so I hadn't managed to finish it yet. It has lovely descriptions of the clothes people wore in London a long time ago. My plan was that if I wrote about the clothes then I'd probably be able to squeeze five hundred words out of my brain, but it was going to be a struggle. If I thought I could get away with it, I'd have drawn Mr Grimpson a picture of the silk dresses instead.

Poor Drusilla. She would easily be able to do Jen's homework for her and save her hair, but who wants to do someone else's work for them? Jen wasn't stupid, but she was lazy. Matthew Fuller once told her that she was such a *total slacker* (that means a complete lazy-bones) that she'd get someone else to wipe her own bum for her if she could. She got her revenge on him by stuffing treacle pudding into his blazer pocket at lunch time. At the time I thought it was hilarious. Now I think he was right about her and the pudding trick was actually really babyish.

So **Cowardly Cordelia** squeezed along the corridor, wishing I could magic myself up to the ceiling and swing along the light shades to get as far as possible from the girls' toilets, the scene of my crime. When I reached the science lab I thought about what a horrid person I'd been when I was friends with Jen and Angela and how I must still be pretty horrid now, if I could see someone being bullied like that, even Drusilla, and not do anything to stop it.

I used to be one of the kids who teased Drusilla about her hair and her American accent and her extra brain, which we thought she must carry in one of the two backpacks she always had with her. She carried one on the front and one on the back, both full of stuff. The one she wore on the front was full of medicines – we'd discovered this fact when Jen had nicked it. It was almost a portable branch of Boots, with her inhaler and all sorts of vitamins inside. She got it all back, but then we tried to do things just to set off her allergies, like throwing mown grass at her from the playing field to make her sneeze or trying to get her to have milk, which gave her asthma, or peanuts, which could kill her. We were just HORRIBLE.

I used to think that people like Jen and Angela were winners and, even though I was beginning to realise what COMPLETE LOSERS they really were, I was also thinking that it might be safer to try and hang out with them again rather than risk being bullied, like Drusilla. Like I said, I was **Cowardly Cordelia**.

But then I sat down in the science lab and remembered that Drusilla and I both now had EMPTY SEAT SYNDROME. I hope you've never experienced this. It's when the seat next to yours is ALWAYS empty after nearly everyone has arrived for class. And who should arrive last of all but Drusilla, and the only empty seat was next to YOURS TRULY.

Mrs Duvall was surprised.

'It's not like you to be late, Drusilla. Come along, sit down next to Cordelia.'

The ONLY thing I could think of that Drusilla Drummond-Steinway and I had in common was that no one sat next to us. To fully understand my MORTIFICATION at having to sit next to her, you have to grasp the level of her dorkiness. Drusilla D-S is the ONE and ONLY person I have ever seen play the saxophone and NOT look cool. HOW can you NOT look cool playing the sax? Now do you understand?

It was hard to put your finger on why nobody

liked Drusilla. Being uncool as described above is one reason, but being a PERMANENT outcast, like she was, meant that there had to be other reasons. Maybe it was the way she knew the answer to every question, and ALWAYS put her hand up. She didn't keep quiet about her genius; she just let her hand keep popping up, like something had bitten her in the armpit, not even giving it a rest when the teachers said, 'All right, Drusilla, let's give someone else a turn, shall we?'

Or it could have been her irritating, squeaky voice, or the fact that her accent was so strong that sometimes it was hard to understand her. I don't know. From the outside, there was just something DEEPLY ANNOYING about her and that's enough to get you SERIOUSLY SIDELINED at this school.

At least Drusilla didn't smell bad. She had a fresh, soapy scent. I'll admit that. That prize, the prize for CLASS STINKY PERSON went to Sonya Hardwicke. Fortunately for the rest of us, Sonya stuck, like chewed gum, to Richard Antrobus, who didn't seem to have a sense of smell.

But the damage was done. She had sat down next to me, and I was now paired with Drippy Drusilla on the very first day of term. This humiliation was probably what I deserved, I thought gloomily. It was my punishment for sneaking out of the toilet and leaving her in Jen and Angela's clutches. Drusilla would be right next to me whenever we had the same class, reminding me of what a coward I was. I thought that perhaps I should start trying to get myself expelled. It might be my only escape from this TORTURE.

The term was not starting well.

I managed not to speak to Drusilla much in science. She didn't look as though she'd been crying after her ordeal in the toilets, as far as I could tell. In fact, she looked calm and composed, except when her arm kept shooting up to answer questions. Then she looked like a jack-in-a-box. I wanted to slap her down and nail the lid shut. Mostly, I ignored her but I realised – and THIS was worrying – that she was also ignoring ME.

After lunch we had English, and I had to sit next to her again because I was late. I got lost in a corridor and GENUINELY couldn't find room 213B. Mr Grimpson didn't believe me.

'No excuses, Miss Codd,' he said in a bad-tempered voice. 'Just sit down and stop holding up my lesson.'

Mr Grimpson always used our surnames. He was like a cartoon of an old-fashioned teacher, with his grey moustache and thin hair and green tweed jackets. He even wore corduroy trousers and brown lace-up shoes AND a knitted waistcoat with leather buttons. He belonged in a room full of pipe smoke with an open fire and piles of dusty books. I sometimes wondered if he'd slipped in from another time dimension, or had somehow escaped from a St Trinian's film (the old black and white ones, not the rubbish new ones where the girls are just bitchy and BORING).

Anyhow, I thought it might be interesting to see if I could distract Drusilla and get her into trouble, so I started writing her a note.

Mr Grimpson scrawled a RIDICULOUSLY long and complicated paragraph on the whiteboard in thick, black pen. He snapped instructions at us like he was pretending to be a soldier in charge of other soldiers.

'Right. Find at least *four* verbs in that lot. Four *verbs* and at least *six nouns,* including one *proper* noun, and *three adjectives.* Ten minutes. Work in silence. Off you go.'

Heads went down. When Mr Grimpson told

you to get on with something, you did. I slid the note over to Drusilla.

I suppose you understand all this stuff.

She wrote back. It was working – she was being distracted.

Of course. It's easy. What's your problem?

I heard Drusilla sigh and saw, from the corner of my eye, that she was shaking her head in despair at my OBVIOUS STUPIDITY. I wrote back again.

I'm too busy thinking about something else.

A boy, I suppose.

No, actually. I was remembering a film I watched last night.

I like movies. Which one?

Mr Grimpson began patrolling the classroom. I scribbled back quickly,

I'll tell you after class.

What was I doing, inviting her to speak to me after class? I should dive down the corridor in the opposite direction AS FAST AS POSSIBLE, not risk being seen in conversation with her.

I was too scared to carry on passing notes once Mr Grimpson started patrolling between the tables. Of course, Drusilla found ALL the verbs, nouns and adjectives that he wanted, while I struggled to find half of them. I can speak the English language pretty well, but I get bored STIFF if I have to chop up sentences like vegetables and squash the bits into little bunches called 'verbs' and 'adjectives'. It takes all the fun out of writing things down.

When the lesson was over Drusilla gave me her big, super-eager-to-please smile and looked at me with her chocolate-brown eyes magnified through her glasses. I started making my way to the playground for some air, but she scampered along the corridor beside me like a pestering puppy.

'So, which movie were you thinking about?' she squeaked.

I kept walking, saying, 'Oh, you wouldn't know it. It's an old one.'

She squeaked again, 'Try me. I've seen lots.'

What sort of films would Drusilla be interested in? Probably Disney stuff, I thought, all pink and sugary. Baby films. But my mouth fell open when she said, 'I collect 60's movies. I like gangster films best, but I love all those glamorous old movie stars, too, like Audrey Hepburn in *Breakfast at Tiffany's*.'

I stopped in my tracks and turned to face her.

'You're kidding! That's the film I was thinking about. I watched *Breakfast at Tiffany's* last night for about the zillionth time.'

Drusilla beamed. 'Wow! I have all of Audrey Hepburn's movies.'

Her words hit me like a BIG FAT PUNCH. 'All of them?'

She had ALL of them? I only had three.

She nodded and her glasses slipped down her nose. Drusilla's glasses slipped a lot, like they needed tightening up or she'd borrowed them from someone with a bigger head. 'We have tons of old movies,' she told me. 'We're total film freaks in our house.'

I noticed that when they weren't magnified through lenses, her chocolaty brown eyes were quite pretty. She pushed her glasses back into place and said, 'Maybe you'd like to come over and watch something?'

I think the shock of finding that Drusilla obviously had SOME SORT OF TASTE, although it was well hidden, must have temporarily disturbed my sanity because I heard myself say, 'Thanks. That'd be great.

I could come this evening, if you like.'

WHAT WAS I DOING? My chances of having any normal friends again were sinking like the TITANIC. I would be the only girl NOT allowed into ANY of the lifeboats. No one would want me. If word got around that I'd watched a film with Drusilla, and even been to her dweeb house and met her squeaky-voiced, drippy family, I'd be dead. But I'd said it now, and she was rattling on, bubbling like a little egg boiling in a pan. She looked fit to pop with excitement. I almost felt a bit sorry for her, but not nearly as sorry as I felt for myself.

Conversation started falling out of my mouth. INTERESTED, FRIENDLY conversation. WHAT was going on here!?

'*Breakfast at Tiffany's* is one of my all-time favourite films at the moment,' I said. 'I draw the costumes. That's what I want to do when I'm older, design costumes.'

I WAS OPENING MY SECRETEST DREAMS TO THE SCHOOL WEIRDY-CHILD! I couldn't stop myself – it just tumbled out. Drusilla looked delighted, as if no one had ever told her anything private before.

She nodded slowly, saying, 'That's *so* cool,'

which made her glasses slip again. She shoved them back, adding, 'I don't know what I'm gonna be yet.'

As I sat on the bus later (yes, I actually got a seat that day), breathing in the smelly air, I felt sick. It wasn't the bus smells that made me want to throw up, but the thought that I might spend the rest of my school life being stalked by Drusilla. Or was it, I wondered, even worse than that? Did I have an INNER-GEEK who wouldn't be trapped inside me any longer? Was I, perhaps, going to turn into a girl LIKE Drusilla but with a much smaller brain? Was it possible, even, that we were destined to become friends?

6

Mum's friend Maggie was visiting her that evening.
A lot of Mum and Dad's friends had stopped coming
to see them when they had to sell the restaurant,
but Maggie stuck by Mum and came round quite
often. She stuck by Mum when Dad left, too. I liked
Maggie. She was big and laughed a lot, which made
her chunky jewellery jangle, and she had long, curly
silver hair like a fairy godmother might have. She and
Mum had worked together at the office for Mr Snaul.
It was a company that rented out massive lorries. The
lorries moved big loads of stuff around the country:
tons of breakfast cereal, plant pots, vegetables, shoes,
clothes – just about anything that needed taking to a
shop somewhere. Not many women worked at the

company so Maggie and Mum became good friends. She and Mum were into DEEP GOSSIP MOOD all evening so Mum didn't mind when I asked if I could go to Dru's for a while. I'd sort of hoped that she WOULD mind, so that I could back out. NO SUCH LUCK.

Drusilla's house was only ten minutes' walk from mine, closer to the park and further from the main road, which made it a bit posher than our end of the estate. I didn't really want to be going anywhere because it was so cold outside, and definitely not to her house. I could've been in my cosy room, watching *Gone with the Wind* and practising drawing those enormous silk skirts with hooped petticoats underneath that Vivien Leigh wears. But I put on everything woolly that I could find and stomped off into the dark.

I suspected that I was in for a really RUBBISH time listening to Drusilla jabbering on about boring stuff. If her story about having loads of good films was made up, just to try and make me interested in being her friend, then I was ready to start a row with her and clear off at the FIRST opportunity.

A woman opened the door who had the same wild, mousey-brown hair as Drusilla, but it was pinned up. Little curly bits escaped here and there and she had blonde highlights, which looked good. I guessed this must be Drusilla's mum and I was surprised. I'd expected her to look old and boring, or like a freaky old witch, but DEFINITELY NOT pretty, like this lady.

'Well, hi,' she said, beaming at me with perfect teeth. 'You must be Cordelia. Come on in. I'm Liz, Dru's mom.'

I thought Dru sounded SO much nicer than Drusilla that I decided to start calling her that, too. Dru's mum shook my hand, which was something not many people had done before. Thankfully, I'd seen enough people shake hands in films to know how it was done properly. You have to look into the other person's eyes and shake firmly but without squeezing too hard.

Her mum had the same accent as Dru, but her voice didn't squeak like Dru's. Instead it was soft and interesting. I stepped inside and looked around. Everything was clean and bright. Dru's mum leaned upstairs and called, 'Hey, Dru! Cordelia's here.'

Dru appeared at the top of the stairs, smiling.

'Hi! Come up.'

Now, if I'd been Dru I would've been a bit nervous in case my new friend (me) hadn't turned up, or else I would've been panicking about how I was going to write Jen's essay for her and save myself from having my hair chopped off. Dru, however, didn't seem to have a care in the world. Her mum called again as I made my way upstairs.

'Shall I bring some cookies up?'

Dru grinned, dangling over the banisters, her hair a storm cloud of frizziness.

'Yeah, please, and hot chocolate. Want some hot chocolate, Cordelia?'

I nodded. 'Yes, please.'

'Coming up!' Dru's mum chirped, like a cheerful waitress.

Dru's room wasn't much bigger than mine, but she had a desk in front of the window with a huge laptop on it. The same space in my room was filled by my sewing machine and piles of fabric and patterns and thread. My bed was quite small, but Dru had an enormous double that almost filled the rest of the space, and there were shelves and shelves of books and films.

'Great room,' I said, looking around for something

that would put me off becoming her friend, but only seeing things that I liked and wished that I had myself.

'Thanks. It's kind of small compared to back home, but it's fine.'

'In America, you mean?'

'Yep.' She sat on her swivel chair by the computer, spun it around to face me and patted the bed, inviting me to sit down, which I did. Her bed was really comfy.

'Whereabouts in America did you live?' I asked, expecting her to be from some tiny place where everyone wore overalls and played the banjo.

'I'll show you.'

She swivelled back to face her laptop, pressed a few buttons and brought up a satellite map. I recognised the shape of the USA. She zoomed in, in, in, in again, onto a city on the west coast called Seattle. Then she zoomed out again so that we could see the distance between her old home and her new one. I tried to imagine what it was like in this place called Seattle, but I had no idea. I only knew that there were girls like Dru there.

I have two lists in my head: one list of places that sound glamorous and interesting, that I WILL DEFINITELY visit one day; and one list of places to avoid because they will probably be dull. Right then, I put Seattle on the list of places to avoid, which just shows how STUPID I can be. I didn't know then that Seattle is a really cool city – bigger and more exciting than ANYWHERE I'd ever visited.

'Do you miss it?' I asked.

'Seattle?' Dru shrugged. 'Sometimes.'

She didn't mention it again. Maybe she missed it a LOT and didn't want to start BLUBBING in front of me about all the amazing friends she'd left behind. Or maybe she didn't want me to know that back home in America she was also a FRIENDLESS FREAK.

I checked out the books on Dru's shelves. Most of them were new to me, but I spotted at least four of the titles Mr Grimpson had recommended for our Christmas holiday reading, so that we could write THE DREADED ESSAY! Seeing those books gave me an idea. Maybe, I thought, if I confessed about what I'd seen in the toilets Dru would be SO angry that I hadn't stuck up for her that she'd start an argument. Then I could get out of being friends with her.

'Dru, I saw you in the toilets the other day.'

Dru turned away from the computer to look at me. 'What was I doing? Something embarrassing?'

How could she have forgotten?

'No, no. I mean I saw Jen and Angela bullying you about Mr Grimpson's essay. I saw them and I heard everything.'

She looked shocked.

'You heard all that?'

I just nodded. An argument was coming; I could feel it. Any moment now she would shout at me and I'd use it as an excuse to storm off home.

'You know Jen and Angela aren't my friends at the moment, don't you?' I said.

Dru laughed. 'Wow, yes. I heard you giving her a good yelling down that day.' She flipped her hand, like she was batting a fly away. 'She deserved it. She's SO spoiled.'

That wasn't what I expected.

'Oh. You heard our argument?'

'Yeah, EVERYONE heard it. It was great. You maybe shouldn't have called her fat, but the rest was right on target.'

It was my turn to look shocked.

'Did other people think it was great, or just you?'

Dru gave another one of her shrugs and stuck out her bottom lip.

'Some of them did. Who cares?'

I cared. I cared a LOT about what other people

thought of me and of what I did and said, and who was my friend. Maybe I cared too much.

'You were just being honest,' Dru went on. 'You don't fit in with those two, anyway. I never thought you did.'

She never thought I did? SHE? Dru had an opinion about MY social life?! I hadn't thought of this before. I suddenly dropped the idea of starting an argument and running home because I was curious to know what other opinions she might have about school.

'Was I ever as horrible to you as Jen and Angela are?' I asked, hoping she'd say no.

Dru shrugged again. Did she shrug everything off?

'You were kind of *mean* sometimes, but new kids with different accents always get a hard time at first, don't they? And I'm tougher than I look. Besides, I know it's not me that has the problem. It's the ones who do the mean stuff that have *personal problems.*'

This was a new idea to me, but Dru was ABSOLUTELY RIGHT. I had a COMPLETELY messed-up family, Jen had her control-freak dad, and Angela was terrified of Jen so she did whatever she was told. We all picked on Dru because WE were unhappy. And Dru clearly didn't give a MONKEY NUT about what girls like us thought of her. How did she manage THAT? At Beckmere EVERYONE cared about EVERY LITTLE THING. Everything was either a reason to hate someone, or to bully them, or to be their friend, or to stop being their friend. EVERY LITTLE THING was a great big DRAMA-RAMA to most of Year 7, but not to Dru.

I suddenly heard myself apologising.

'I'm sorry for the times I was horrid to you. You didn't deserve it.'

It just came out of my mouth. I'd come here to prove that Dru was too weird to hang out with and now, after five minutes' conversation, I found myself saying sorry to her and actually WANTING her to like me. I was still very cautious, though. If she started being as annoying at home as she was at school, I'd drop her like a hot cowpat.

Dru rolled her eyes and tutted.

'It's history. OK? Can we just get on and watch a movie now?'

She got up from her seat and started pulling DVDs off the shelf and chucking them on the bed.

'What about the essay thing with Jen, though?'

I asked. 'What will you do about that?'

She spread the films out so that I could read the titles.

'Look, if Jen thinks I'm going to be her substitute brain she's even dumber than she looks. On Wednesday she'll ask me for the essay. I won't have it, of course, and I'll tell her I'm not going to do it.'

'But she said she'd cut your hair off!'

Dru paused and looked at me like I was crazy. 'Do you really think she'd *dare*?'

'YES,' I said, nodding, with my eyes popping wide.

Dru shook her head calmly and pulled out another film. 'I don't,' she said. 'And if she *does* I'll go to Mr Grimpson with my handfuls of hair and you can be my witness that it was Jen who chopped it off. Who do you think will be in the biggest trouble? By the time she's allowed back into school my hair will have grown again.'

'You really ARE tough, aren't you?' I said, genuinely impressed.

Dru sniffed, like it was nothing, like it was normal to be that brave.

'When you're a geeky freak like me you've got

to hold your ground, or you get squished. Right?'

Wow! Drusilla Drummond-Steinway had turned out to be a COMPLETE surprise!

7

People soon started to see me talking to Dru at school and I knew that if I WAS going to be friends with her I'd have to COMPLETELY let go of the idea that I could get back with a NORMAL social group again. It turned out that I didn't really have a choice.

By the end of January I couldn't pretend to myself any longer that I was just testing Dru out to see if she was OK. By then I knew that, although Dru would always be MUCH brainier than me and we didn't like ALL the same things, we did have a great time watching films together and laughed at a lot of the same jokes, and we EVEN liked the same kind of pizza. I just had to face up to the fact that we were ALREADY friends. SO – DECISION MADE. The pair of us slipped RIGHT off the bottom of the cool-to-hang-out-with league tables and became SOCIALLY INVISIBLE. It didn't bother me NEARLY as much as I'd expected – but Jen and Angela soon began making trouble for us.

I'd started going to Dru's place quite a lot. One Sunday afternoon we'd had a great time watching *Roman Holiday* on Dru's laptop. I had taken my sketchbook over and had shown her how I try to draw the costumes. She'd been REALLY impressed so I'd let her keep one of my best drawings of the strappy sandals that Audrey Hepburn wears when she's walking around Rome pretending not to be a princess.

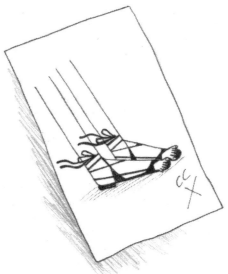

But that great Sunday with Dru was followed by a MISERABLE MONDAY. We were in the toilets at morning break time, just before our science lesson. It had been weeks since Jen had tried to get Dru to do her essay for her, and Dru had been right. Jen had backed off when she'd refused to do it. But she'd sworn she'd have her revenge, and this looked like the day.

I was waiting for Dru to finish washing her hands. She was explaining the science homework to me, saying that osmosis was 'really easy' to understand and that she'd show me a website where I could watch it happening on film. Jen and Angela came in just then and stood, smiling nastily at both of us as if they'd just caught something in a trap that they intended to kill.

'Just look at her,' said Jen, walking over and tugging my ponytail HARD so that it hurt. 'She's really let herself go, and she's got her pet weirdo with her.'

Dru picked up her bag saying, 'Let's go, Cordelia. We don't have to listen to this.'

But Jen put a hand on Dru's shoulder to stop her and said in a hissy-snake voice, 'You owe me an essay, freak.'

'I told you already,' said Dru, keeping her cool, 'I'm *never* doing your homework for you. Try growing a brain of your own.'

Jen shoved Dru into a cubicle and grabbed her bag. Angela giggled and narrowed her eyes at me, daring me to interfere. Jen was rummaging through Dru's stuff while Dru picked herself up off the cubicle floor.

'How about I flush your work down the toilet?' Jen said. 'Just so that you know you can't mess about with me?'

I couldn't stand still and let Jen and Angela treat Dru like this again, could I? And besides, my ponytail hurt where she'd tugged it. I GRABBED the bag back off Jen and put it behind me on the floor. She turned on me, hissing like a snake again.

'Sticking up for your dorky little mate, are you, Cordelia? How's your dad, by the way? Not come home yet? I don't blame him.'

That pushed **ALL** my buttons at once. I shoved Jen into the next cubicle so hard that she sat down with a bump onto the toilet. I lifted her ankles and she slid back, getting her bum wedged in the toilet bowl. Then I flushed the loo. The back of her skirt would be soaking wet and she'd have to walk around all day looking like she'd peed herself. She SHRIEKED, of course, but I ignored her. Dru and I left her there and headed for science. Angela had disappeared.

'Thanks, Cordelia,' Dru panted as we elbowed our way along the crowded corridor. 'I forgot that she'd probably come back for revenge.'

'I don't think she's finished with us yet,' I warned her.

8

By February Dru and I were best friends and it looked like we'd stay that way. Dad showed no signs of coming back and I'd almost got used to it being just me and Mum. The terrible Christmas with Granny Twigg was also almost forgotten. Things SHOULD have been settling down, but instead they took a sharp nosedive towards DISASTER.

Mum was working overtime quite a bit at the office to make some extra money. She was also doing ALL the stuff that Dad used to do

AND trying to give me extra treats to make up for him not being there

AND trying to not let me see how sad she was underneath it all. I helped around the house as much as I could, but sometimes I got things wrong and made a mess, and then Mum got more stressed.

One evening Mum asked if I'd mind if she went out. This sounded great – Mum going out and relaxing, but I thought she meant with Maggie. When the doorbell rang I went into SHOCK-HORROR-PARALYSIS. It was her boss, Mr Snaul, who'd come to take her out.

SNAULUS THE WALRUS

He stood on the doorstep, grinned at me and said, 'Call me Terry, sweetheart.'

NOT FLAMING LIKELY, I thought.

He filled our tiny hallway with his big belly and the smell of something out of an aerosol can. I followed Mum upstairs after she'd called to him, 'Take a seat, Terry. I'll only be a minute,' in a voice that was so yuckily sweet that it made me feel sick.

I left him in the living room. I did **NOT** want to be alone with him for a NANOSECOND. I leaned against Mum's dressing table, watching her put lipstick on – the shiny toffee-coloured one that I liked to borrow.

'I don't like him. He's really FAT,' I whispered.

'That's a bit unkind, Coco. Looks aren't everything.

Surely I've brought you up to understand that much.'

Well, yes, of course she had. I knew better, but I couldn't possibly be reasonable at a time like this. The situation was too DREADFUL AND DRASTIC for politeness. This was a **CRISIS**. Did she want to go out with someone who looked completely the opposite of Dad just for the contrast? Dad was skinny, despite all the cooking and eating he did, and he was going bald, so he shaved his hair really short.

But Mr Snaul had thick, wavy hair that he put some sort of GLOOP on to make it shiny – not like old-fashioned film stars, however, not by a million miles. There was nothing Clark Gable or Omar Sharif about Terry Snaul. I'm certain he dyed it black, too, because it didn't look quite real. It was like a dark jelly sitting on his head.

YUCK. Jelly head.

I shuddered as I thought that perhaps it might be a wig,

a rug

a toupee

a slaphead slipover

a carpet flap.

Of all the names I knew for a man-wig, none

of them could ever be considered *remotely glamorous*.

A volcano of horror bubbled up in me as I imagined all sorts of terrible things Mum and Mr Snaul might do. They might even dance at a nightclub. This is the sort of **HIDEOUS SPECTACLE** that grown-ups should NOT make of themselves, and absolutely NO ONE should dance with MY MUM, except maybe my dad, who's quite a good dancer…but only if they're a tiny bit sloshed AND it's a special occasion, like a wedding.

Snaulus the Walrus's wig would DEFINITELY fall off if they danced. It would flop on the floor and get trampled by other dancers. It would be just AWFUL and *desperately unglamorous* and Mum would try to say something to make him feel better. She would probably have to say, 'Don't worry, you're much more handsome without it,' or 'Wig, *schmigg*, leave it where it is. You don't need it now you've got me.'

Mum was too kind.

She would get stuck with him because she's a softy, and before I knew it he'd be expecting me to call him Dad.

UNTHINKABLE!

My mind was full of these HORRENDOUS possibilities. I HAD to prevent what felt like an INEVITABLE AND LONG-TERM DISASTER.

I went on at Mum as she was putting last-minute things into her handbag, her best one that had a lovely catch that clicked when you shut it – the one she only used when Dad took her somewhere elegant. She looked lovely in her best dress. I'd helped her choose it in the shop. It made her look like Rita Hayworth because it crossed over at the front and had tiny gathers on the shoulders. I couldn't stand the thought of her preening and prettifying herself for someone who wasn't my dad, even though Dad had been DESPICABLE to both of us. The feelings got confused and I didn't know who to be angry with.

'He smells of NASTY aftershave,' I said to Mum.

I let Mum see me shiver with disgust. I knew I had a snooty look on my face but I just had to make sure she knew how UTTERLY disapproving I was, in the hope that she'd come to her senses.

'I can't believe my mum would be seen out with someone so SLIPPERY looking.'

Mum sighed and smiled, like it was a pain in the bum to have to listen to me.

'It's just a nice change for me to be taken out.'

She shook her head. 'It's not serious.'

'He looks like a WALRUS with no tusks.'

'And I say to you again, *young lady*, that looks aren't everything.'

'But I don't like him.'

'You don't *know* him, yet. How can you judge him like that?'

My eyes popped and my voice squeaked as I whispered angrily, 'YET? That means you're already planning to see him lots more.'

Mum clicked her handbag shut. I noticed she'd painted her nails, too. A beautiful shell pink that looked so pretty with her green dress.

'That's to be decided. You might like him if you try to get to know him.'

'I don't want to **KNOW** him,
and I will **NEVER** call him **TERRY**
and he is **NEVER** to call me **SWEETHEART**
again, so please **TELL** him.'

Then Mum got cross. She didn't shout; she just raised her voice to a hard sort of whisper and her cheeks flushed like grumpy roses. She pulled her coat off the hanger, her best coat, the black wool one with the fake fur round the collar that I couldn't wait to grow into. She slung it over her arm.

'You're being selfish, Coco. It's *my* business who takes me out. We're only going to have dinner. It's not as if he's a proper boyfriend.'

I let her walk past me, but had to say, quickly, right in her ear, 'AND his hair isn't real, y'know? It'll fall off in his soup, I bet. You just see. And his teeth will get left behind in a bread roll. I'm right. I KNOW I'm right. He WON'T DO. He'll **NEVER** do. He's not NEARLY sophisticated enough for us.'

Perhaps I was suffering from a case of BRAT SHOCK. That's when I know I'm being OUTRAGEOUSLY AWKWARD but I'm so scared of things not going right that I try to control Mum by getting into a NARKY-KNICKERS FIT.

I knew that she was perfectly entitled to be taken out for dinner, but there would've been something slimy about Mr Snaul even if he'd looked like a gorgeous film star, even like George Peppard. My creepiness detector was BLARING like an ambulance siren, and I was terrified that Mum didn't hear it, too.

Adults can be SO dim at choosing each other. They need our guidance.

That night, while Mum was out with the Walrus, I ate a giant pot of yoghurt all by myself.

It was black cherry flavour.
I will NEVER eat black cherry yoghurt again.
It tastes of the STUPIDITY of adult behaviour.

9

Mum came home earlier than I'd expected. My evening had been spent watching rubbish on television, feeling too grouchy about Mum going out with Snaulus the Walrus to concentrate on anything useful. The danger of my mother falling in love with a LARGE SEA MAMMAL was too disturbing for me to think straight. My homework had been abandoned and I couldn't even bring myself to put on a film and draw dresses. I switched off *Celebrity Garden Makeover*, or whatever mind-mashing RUBBISH it was that I'd been staring at, when I heard her key scrape in the door. She didn't call 'Hi' all cheery and smiley. This was a GOOD sign.

Maybe Snaulus had been TERMINALLY

BORING or burped loudly at the dinner table or licked his plate. Perhaps my wig fantasy had become a gruesome reality and she was feeling shy with embarrassment because I'd been proved right, after all.

Mum went straight into the kitchen. I heard her put the kettle on and followed her. She didn't say anything, just sat down to wait for the water to boil and looked at me, sighing. I started to feel worried when I noticed that her eyes were red and watery.

'What happened, Mum?'

She shook her head and reached for a box of tissues that was at the end of the table. She pulled a couple out, dabbed her eyes and blew her nose. I sat down opposite her, frowning.

'What? Mum?'

She breathed in slowly before speaking. 'Well. I don't think you need worry about Terry becoming my boyfriend.'

My shoulders relaxed and I slouched back in the chair. WHAT A RELIEF! But I sat upright again straight away, not feeling so sure. 'WHY don't I need to worry?'

'Well. Let's just say that he…he didn't behave very well.'

I went scarlet and pressed my lips together. I knew that meant he'd done something VERY BAD INDEED. I imagined him grabbing at my mum with his big pudgy hands. It made me **SICK** and **BOILING**.

'I hope you **KICKED** him where it **HURTS**,' I said. 'I hope you pulled his wig off.'

Mum looked surprised. Then she laughed a little bit.

'No, Coco, that wasn't necessary. I just thanked him for dinner and said that I didn't think it would be appropriate for me to go out with him again. Then I left.'

WHAT? My head was full of blood-curdling revenge. 'Why didn't you get ANGRY with him?'

'Because I prefer to stay calm when I can and just point things out, not shout or hit people.'

'DAD would've hit him.'

Mum smiled again, and sort of frowned at the same time, like I'd confused her. 'If your dad were here I wouldn't be going out for dinner with someone else, would I?'

I realised what a STUPID thing I'd said. We looked at each other for a second while it sank in, then Mum came round the table and hugged me.

'Bowl of cornflakes?' she suggested.

I nodded.

'And some hot chocolate, please.'

We ended up laughing and giggling about how DEATHLY DULL Snaulus the Walrus had been.

Mum said he'd talked about caravans all evening.

CARAVANS! OK, lots of people like them, but *PLEASE!* Where's the glamour?

We went to bed quite happy, but Snaulus the Walrus turned out to be a really BAD LOSER.

All through February, March and most of April, Mum started coming home later and later. She was given tons of extra work to do at the office by YOU-KNOW-WHO. Sometimes she rang and asked me to start the dinner. She whispered instructions in case Snaulus heard her making what he said was a 'personal call'.

Chop one of those.
Boil one of these.
Slice an onion.
I should be home by seven.

The dinner never tasted like much in particular when I'd cooked it. Some nights I ate mine before Mum got home because I was hungry and couldn't wait. Hours later, she would stagger through the door, drop her bag in the hall and sit staring at her plate, too tired to eat. She was getting pale and spotty and didn't bother with lipstick any more.

We hardly ever got time to talk.

In the mornings, she had to leave before me, and if we flopped in front of the television together at night she would be asleep in five minutes. The washing-up got left for two or three days at a time, going crusty in the sink.

'Can't they get someone else to do this extra work?' I asked her as I was pouring milk onto bedtime cornflakes. 'Why do YOU have to stay at the office and do it all?'

Mum was having cereal, too. She shook her head. 'I've asked Terry, but I don't like to pester him.'

My lip curled up in a silent SNARL at the mention of his name. Mum went on.

'I've asked him loads of times, but he ignores me.'

Why didn't she stick up for herself?

'MUM! That's not FAIR. I bet he's doing it on purpose because you don't want to go out with him.'

Mum didn't look up. 'I don't think so, Coco. That would be childish.'

I wasn't convinced.

'He can't be horrible to you just because you don't want to be his girlfriend.'

She shook her head, but still didn't look up from her cereal bowl. She concentrated on scraping the last few cornflakes off the sides with her spoon. 'I don't think he'd do that, Coco.'

I got the feeling that she knew he WOULD do EXACTLY that, but she was scared to admit that he was being a bully. I went on at her again.

'You've got to tell him that you can't do so much work.'

Mum stood up slowly and put her bowl and spoon in the sink, saying, 'I know, Coco. I know.'

But she said it like she didn't have any energy left to argue with him.

Over the next few weeks Mum got more and more tired. We began to argue about stupid things, like where she'd put stuff.

Have you seen this?
Have you seen that?
I know I left it here.
I'm sure I put it there.

We rowed REALLY badly when she went to parents' evening in April and found out how much homework I'd not handed in. She was FURIOUS. You might think that hanging around with Dru would make me work a bit harder, but when Dru went home to get her homework done I would flop down and watch a film and start drawing. It took my mind off how much I missed Dad. Then Mum might ring and give me a list of jobs to do around the house because she had to stay late at work and my homework got scribbled at the last minute or forgotten completely.

After the parents' evening I heard Mum crying. She cried quite often, but only when she didn't think I could hear. This time I thought it was because of my school report so I went into her room and said I was sorry and that I'd try to catch up and wouldn't watch any films until I had. She hugged me and said it wasn't that.

'I know you'll work hard. You've been helping a lot in the house and you shouldn't have to do that. It's not your fault, sweetheart. I'm just tired. I'll be fine with a good night's sleep.'

But she wasn't.

A couple of weeks after that, at the end of April, Mum had to stop work completely because she was FRAZZLED OUT. She went to bed with some tablets from Dr Khan and hardly got up again for weeks.

Dru was visiting her family in Seattle for the Easter Holidays, so she had no idea that my life was falling apart while she was away. I missed her SO much.

One of the few things Mum got out of bed for was Dad's phone calls. I stopped answering the phone in case it was him. When Mum shouted up the stairs, 'D'you want a chat with Dad, Coco?' I would yell over the banisters, '**NO!**' and then slam my bedroom door as loudly as I could so that he'd hear it all the way down in London. How could he **NOT** be here when we needed him to help us so much now that Mum was poorly?

I DID want to talk to him, of course, but I wanted to talk to him EVERY DAY, not just when he found time to ring. I wanted to talk to him at meal times and out in the garden and at the supermarket or the library, not over the phone.

I did **NOT** want a **TELEPHONE PARENT**.

If I started talking to him on the phone I'd
end up letting him convince me that some sort of
HALFWAY arrangement was OK. Then I'd end up
being shuffled back and forth in the holidays and
seeing 'patches' of parents. Well, some kids might be
OK with that, but not me.

I wanted the whole Dad kit or NOTHING.

One thing that I became really good at when Mum got too poorly to work was doing my own laundry. When I had to start looking after Mum AND the house I always made sure that I washed my school stuff regularly. That was my priority job, especially after THE B$_O$G$_E$Y INCIDENT.

It wasn't that Mum was lazy, it was just as if her battery was completely flat – she had no energy left to do anything. But I was still **SO ANGRY** underneath. **ANGRY** that she was poorly, **ANGRY** that I had a scruffy home, **ANGRY** that I had to do the housework and **ANGRY** most of all because **WHERE WAS MY DAD** when we needed him? My anger came out in explosions now and then and the legendary BOGEY INCIDENT was one of my biggest.

It was the beginning of May and Jen was hanging around with Ellie Simmons now, the snootiest girl in the UNIVERSE. Angela had been elbowed out of their circle since she'd abandoned Jen in the toilets that day. I saw her sometimes, hanging around with a bunch of quieter girls. Maybe it had been a good thing for her, too, to fall out with Jen.

I was having trouble keeping up with all the jobs I had to do around the house and I'd run out of clean blouses for school. In a mad panic because I was late, I'd grabbed one off the dirty laundry pile. It was REALLY crumpled and scruffy looking, but it didn't smell too bad so it had to do. I thought that if I kept my blazer on no one would notice all the creases, but I'd forgotten about changing for PE. Of course, Jen and Ellie Simmons spotted the crinkled mess I was wearing and Ellie just HAD to say something in her RIDICULOUS – LOUD – *posh* – VOICE.

'LOOK, EVERYBODY,' she squealed. 'Over HERE.'

She pointed to my back as I bent down to sort my socks out and waved EVERYONE towards me. You would hear Ellie's voice, even if you had FOUR

HUNDRED pillows over your head. She sounded like the queen at FIVE MILLION DECIBELS. So, of course, all thirty-five girls in the changing room turned and looked at MY skanky blouse.

'*Look!*' she squawked. 'Coddy Fish Fingers is wearing a *crinkly old handkerchief!*'

Only Ellie Simmons would say '*Hend…ker… chuff*' like she was strangling a sneeze, and with all three syllables, not *hanky* or *snot rag* or *tissue*. Girls peered around the coat stands to look, and laugh. Now that she had an audience, Ellie went on.

'Hend…ker…chuffs are for *bogies*. Here, Coddy, have one of *mine*.'

I couldn't believe it. My jaw dropped. I went into shock. *Posh* Ellie Simmons stuck her finger up her nostril, pulled out a bogey and ACTUALLY WIPED IT ON THE BACK OF MY BLOUSE!

Dru was in shock, too. Her eyes bulged in disbelief.

Some girls said,

'Yuk!' and

'Gross!' and

'That's *disgusting*, Ellie!'

But most of them just screwed up their faces, giggled and looked away.

They soon turned back again.

OK, I KNOW I should have told a teacher, or just wiped it off and played cool, but I was **BOILING** inside, **FOAMING**, like when I tore up Dad's letter and when I yelled at him on the phone, and like when I shoved Jen's bottom down the loo. I called Ellie the **WORST** names I could think of, then grabbed her school bag and emptied it onto the floor. All her belongings – her expensive pens and pencil case, her designer sunglasses, her lip gloss, her bus pass, her money, her keys, her books, her mobile phone and her soppy boyfriend photograph – fell out with a huge CLATTER and slid across the tiles. I knew I was being violent and WAY out of control, but I couldn't stop myself. She grabbed at the empty bag, but I was quicker. I tugged it back, stepped up onto the bench and stuffed it right down over her *posh*, squawky head.

I twizzled the bag round and round so that her hair was all messed up. It probably hurt her ears, but I didn't care – I **WANTED** to hurt her.

Ellie SCREEEAMED! inside the bag.

Miss Haliborn had just gone outside and didn't hear because the bag muffled Ellie's WAILING. Girls stared, their eyes popping like ping-pong balls.

When I let Ellie go she staggered about for a few seconds, like she'd just come off a fairground ride. I grabbed her stupid **TOP-SECRET-GIRLS-ONLY-DIARY** and wiped the bogey off on its sequined cover.

'Just returning what's yours,' I said.

She'd NEVER pick THAT off!

Then I carried on dressing as if nothing had happened.

Luckily for me, Miss Haliborn walked in before Ellie and Jen could think of anything to do to me in return, but UNLUCKILY, all Miss Haliborn saw was Ellie, looking a COMPLETE WRECK, scrabbling about under the bench for the contents of her bag. She made whimpering sounds like a lost puppy. Did I care?

NO!

Then Ellie used her most PATHETIC voice. 'Miss Haliborn, can you *do* something about Cordelia, *please?*' She looked up from the floor as if I'd pushed her there. 'She's ruining things for *everyone* again.'

Loads of girls saw the whole thing, but they sided with Ellie, NATURALLY. NATURALLY, because she had a reputation for making people's lives difficult and also NATURALLY, because she was allowed to have parties that they all wanted to be invited to because Ellie had a brother in Year Ten with lots of good-looking mates. Miss Haliborn glared at me. I didn't get a chance to explain.

'Cordelia Codd. Outside. *Now.*'

Dru suddenly snapped out of her frozen-with-shock position next to me.

'I saw what happened, Miss Haliborn. I'm a witness. Cordelia didn't start it.'

She followed me outside, but Miss Haliborn turned on her.

'I'm surprised at you, Drusilla. I thought you would choose your friends more carefully. Go back to class and think hard before you keep company with this one again.'

'But, Miss Hal–'

Dru had no chance. Miss Haliborn's eyes flared like a witch. 'Go! Now!'

Dru gave me a worried look. 'Good luck,' she whispered.

I refused to apologise to Ellie. Miss Haliborn didn't believe the business about the bogey. She ACTUALLY said, 'A nice girl like Ellie would *never* do anything *so disgusting*.'

'Oh yes she would,' I said. 'You're just pretending she wouldn't because her dad gave the school lots of netballs and gym mats AND because she's good at swimming and you want her in the team to win a trophy so the parents will all think that Beckmere's a wonderful school and send their other kids here.'

That made things worse, of course. Detention all week.

MAJOR STRESS.

Sometimes there is NO JUSTICE.

Dru waited for me every evening. We walked home together and I realised that this is what REAL friends do. They stick by you when you've done something stupid. But they don't pretend that you were right; they're just there for you.

If Mum had known what had really happened, she'd have thrown a BAD ONE, so I pretended that I was late after school every day because the buses had been full, or that I had to go to the library, or that I was getting help with my homework from Dru. I hated lying to her, but I wanted to protect her from getting even more upset. I don't know if it was the right thing to do. I mean, what would you have done?

In the evenings, I went to see Dru whenever I thought Mum would be OK on her own for a while. Her family knew that Mum was poorly and they were very kind about it. Dru's mum sometimes gave me cakes or soup to take home.

I really liked being inside Dru's house. It reminded me that our house used to be full of fun. But I could see, by looking at Dru's mum, how much my own mum's life had gone downhill.

How was I going to help Mum get better quickly so that things could be normal again? I often cried on the way home because all the things that had disappeared from my home were still at Dru's house: light, smiles, clean and shiny rooms, lovely cooking smells. Our house had become stuffy, dark and grim, with its curtains always shut and the paint peeling off. Mum's friend Maggie was our only regular visitor. She always helped to tidy up a bit, but it soon got untidy again. I didn't want anyone else to see what it was like, so I vowed that Drusilla must NEVER come to our house.

12

Dru and I didn't get much bother after the BOGEY INCIDENT. Bullies were afraid they'd get the 'Ellie treatment', as it became known. I wasn't particularly proud of the fact that kids were frightened of my temper, but it kept Ellie and Jen away. Unfortunately it kept a lot of other people away, too. Only Dru stuck by me.

Things suddenly started to look a lot better about two weeks after the Ellie incident, when I bumped into Dean Frampton in the corridor. I mean literally, ABSOLUTELY bumped into him – or his guitar, anyway. He was carrying it over his shoulder and when he turned around to look at something (Alison McDonald's bum, I think) it knocked me flying.

I was taking my latest detention slip to Mr Grimpson in the staffroom for him to sign, but I dropped it when the guitar hit me and had to lie flat down on the dusty floor to get it back from under a row of lockers. I was in this not very elegant position when Dean realised what he'd done and came back to help.

'Whoops-a-daisy. Sorry,' he said.

'Whoops-a-daisy' didn't really fit with his Rock God image, but he had a way of saying it that sounded quite smoochy.

Dean gave me his KILLER smile. It reminded me of a scene in *Gone with the Wind* where Clark Gable smiles at Vivien Leigh like he's a fox about to eat a chicken. But STUPID me didn't think of a fox and a chicken at the time, did I? I just thought how great it was to be helped up by the Year Ten heartthrb and have a smile from him that was just for me.

'OK?' he asked.

He was still smiling. I felt a definite flutter in my stomach when he held my hand and pulled me up.

'Yes, I'm fine. Just dropped my detention slip. Got it now.'

I waved the slip like a little flag. WHY DID I

DO THAT? He knew what a detention slip looked like, for goodness' sake. I gave a stupid little laugh that made me cringe inside and feel like a MORON. He squinted at my face. I thought there must be something stuck to it, a bit of the chocolate bar I'd had earlier, perhaps, but then I realised he'd recognised me.

'You're Drusilla's friend, aren't you? I've seen you two in the canteen together.'

He ran his fingers through his blond hair. He did that to make the bit at the front fall forward again. That's what boys with thick, floppy hair do when they want to flirt with you. They push it back, knowing perfectly well that it'll fall forward again and look cute. How many actors had I seen do THAT? Was Dean Frampton FLIRTING with ME?

'How do you know Dru?' I asked, trying not to keep grinning at him and wishing, OH WISHING, that Jen or Ellie or Angela and her new mates would walk past and see me chatting with Dean.

'Her sister, Jess, just joined the band. She's our new singer,' Dean explained.

A few months ago I would've found it hard to imagine anyone from Drusilla's gene pool singing with a rock band as wild as A&E (Accident and

Emergency). The last lead singer had looked like a model and had an INCREDIBLE voice. That was before I met Jess. She was *gorgeous*. I took a long, hard look at Dru that evening and realised that she wasn't going to look like a geek for much longer. Once she got some trendy glasses, did something with her hair and grew a few centimetres, she was going to be nearly as good-looking as her big sister.

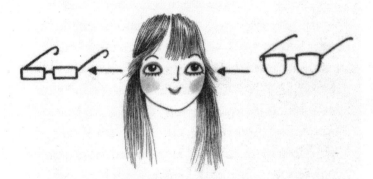

Dean nodded slowly, looking me up and down but not saying anything, which I thought was a bit creepy, but I forgave him.

I had to run and told him so. If I didn't hand the detention slip in by midday it would be doubled to four evenings. Getting detention hadn't been fair. It was just because I'd stamped on Ahmed's toe a little bit. He deserved a lot worse for deleting my work off the computer when I went to the loo. And HOW was I to know that he had an ingrowing toenail?

I was halfway down the corridor when Dean called back.

'Coming to the gig on Friday?'

I shook my head.

I'd already been to Dru's house two nights that week and Mum needed some company because Maggie was on holiday. Mum was extra stressy and tired this week because Dad had called a couple of days ago and she'd cried on the phone. I hadn't known what to do and there was no one there to help me. After Mum had cried, she'd slept and slept, but I hadn't been able to sleep AT ALL. I'd just lain there, getting more angry with Dad again. That's why I'd been in such a bad mood and stamped on Ahmed's foot when he deleted my work.

Dean stretched out his hands like he was begging. 'Come on. It's the finals of Battle of the Bands.' He gave an extra-wide grin. 'We're gonna win.'

I screwed my nose up. I REALLY wanted to go. 'I don't think I can.'

He walked back towards me. 'You could come for pizza with me and the band afterwards.'

My cheeks FIZZED. I was ACTUALLY
sweating a bit, but not in places he could see,
THANK GOODNESS. Dean Frampton was asking
ME out?

I bit my lip. If Mum went to bed early, maybe I
could sneak away. She wouldn't stress MUCH if she
found out. Would she? I managed to sound casual
about it.

'OK. I'll try. I'll see you at the gig if I can make it.'

I deserved an Oscar for my EXTERNAL COOLNESS.
Inside I was sherbet-fizz-giddy with excitement.

This was SO unexpected. It would be
UNBELIEVABLY cool to be seen hanging out with
Dean after the gig. I'd heard older kids talking about
Battle of the Bands. EVERYONE went. It was the
BIG contest between the local schools that was held
every year. Last time A&E came second. Maybe
Dean was right and they WOULD win this one. To
be with Dean, on a date, on the night his band came
first. Now THAT would give me ROCK SOLID
CREDIBILITY. Everyone would want to be my
friend after that. Dru and I would be the *Queens*

of Cool. I felt so special and confident. I thought I would breeze detention.

Instead, I sat in a classroom with a handful of other bored kids. Miss Haliborn hovered around while we did homework or, in my case, while I tried to look like I was thinking about homework but was actually worrying about what I should wear if I COULD get to the Battle of the Bands. There was no money for new things and most of my jeans were getting too short for me.

Dru couldn't meet me after detention that day because of her saxophone lesson AND she was late into school the next day because her allergies had to be checked by the doctor, so I had to wait until the following lunch time to tell her the news.

We were having chips and sausages in the canteen. Dru didn't sound impressed when I told her about Dean. I was SO disappointed. AND she told me that Jess wasn't going to be in A&E after all because she'd already left school and so, according to the rules of Battle of the Bands, it would be cheating.

'And that Dean has a *monster ego*,' she added.

She put her hands to the sides of her head and moved them outwards, blowing her cheeks out at the same time. I shrugged off her insult, blinked very slowly to show I didn't care and bit into a chip soaked with ketchup.

'Well, I expect you HAVE to be super confident to be in a rock band.'

'Yeah, sure. But Jess says he pushes the other band members around. She doesn't think they'll stay together much longer.'

I was getting fed up with Dru today. More than fed up. I was starting to feel my temper boil again. I put my fork down to stop myself from poking her with it.

'Are you trying to spoil this for me?'

Dru shook her head and stuck out her bottom lip as she poured a huge vinegar puddle onto her plate.

'No. I'm just trying to warn you that he might not be as good as he looks.'

I prickled. My ONE chance to have a date with someone IMPRESSIVELY good-looking and Dru was acting like the world's most boring mother. There was only one explanation and I spat it out at her.

'You're just JEALOUS.'

She didn't react. HOW did she manage that? If someone got narky with me I always snapped back straight away.

'Not really,' she said calmly. 'I prefer Latin-looking guys like Carlos in Year Nine. Wow!'

She rolled her eyes and pretended to faint. Normally I would have found this funny because Dru did a brilliant 'fake faint'. She used it once in PE so that she didn't have to climb a rope. Miss Haliborn was TOTALLY convinced. But I didn't laugh this time. I was **FUMING** that she'd been so rude about Dean. It felt like she'd slapped me across the face. **OUCH!** And I wasn't going to shrug that off.

'Carlos?! He doesn't even have a neck. He looks like a GIBBON. At least Dean is fully EVOLVED... and he's interesting and I INTEND to go out with him and have a good time...and you ARE jealous!'

Dru just blinked and let me rant and rave at her, then I stormed off, determined not to be her friend ANY MORE. I didn't need a friend who wasn't going to stick by me before my big date. So WHAT if I didn't have any friends again now. Once I'd been seen hanging around with Dean, friends would run towards me. I'd be SO popular.

For the next two whole days Dru and I didn't speak even though we still had to sit next to each other in almost every class. She was just as stubborn as me at keeping silent. I tried to concentrate but I was distracted by thoughts of how different my life was going to be after Friday and my night out with Dean. I saw him in the corridor a couple of times, but he was with his mates and I don't think he spotted me in the crowd. If he had, I'm sure he would have come over for a chat.

13

Mum was fast asleep that Friday evening when I crept out to Battle of the Bands. I had to keep really quiet while I was getting ready so that I didn't wake her up, which was difficult because I needed to open and close lots of cupboards and drawers trying to find SOMETHING to wear. I left her a note just in case she woke up. She sometimes drifted into the kitchen at night, like a ghost, looking for snacks.

The note said,

Just gone to Drusilla's to watch a film. Will be home by 11 p.m.

Coco x

Of course, it was highly unlikely that I'd EVER be going to Drusilla's again, but Mum had no idea that we'd fallen out. If she thought we were still friends I would be able to pretend that I was visiting Dru when I needed a reason not to be at home, like when I was on my future dates with Dean. I know it was TECHNICALLY a bit of a lie, but there's no way Mum would've let me go out with a group of older boys if I'd told her. What could I do? This was essential to rebuilding my social life, but she would NEVER have understood that.

Battle of the Bands was being held in the gym at Allington Grammar. I found my way there OK. It was only a short bus ride. When I arrived, I made sure Ellie and Jen saw me sitting with the other Year Ten kids who were there to support Dean's band, even though they didn't speak to me much.

Four bands were going to play – two from Allington Grammar, one from Roundcliffe Academy and A&E, from Beckmere High. First up was a SERIOUSLY hunky-looking boy band from Allington called QT. It took me a while to work out that QT stood for Queer Tunes.

Small sighs of disappointment came from the girls.

But, hey, I was going for pizza with the best-looking boy at Beckmere later. What did I care?

The crowd loved QT. They were all RIDICULOUSLY good-looking and wore tight white T-shirts and expensive jeans. Even though they only sang covers of famous boy band songs it was obvious that they'd rehearsed A LOT and they REALLY knew how to sing. First up and they got a standing ovation! They were going to be difficult to follow.

The Roundcliffe band were next. What a contrast! They had huge red mohicans and knee-length Doc Martens and called themselves THE PUSTULES. One of them wore a kilt with a green fur fabric sporran, which I thought looked pretty good. Unfortunately for them, their music was a bit too SHOUTY for most people's taste. Only a group of Roundcliffers with similar haircuts jumped about and applauded.

The second band from Allington took over from THE PUSTULES. Allington boys always had expensive equipment because most of them had loads of dosh. This group, PSYCHODELICIOUS (rubbish name, I thought), had REALLY flashy guitars and a synthesiser that was nearly as big as a bus. I could tell that they'd got their outfits from vintage shops, so they scored high with me for COSTUME EFFORT, but they sang really badly and with miserable looks on their faces. Their music was mostly 80s pop songs, which only seemed to have about three notes. The keyboard player just pressed a few buttons on the synthesiser and the guitarist hardly moved his fingers at all. I thought they were a bit boring, but most of the parents and teachers in the audience loved them. I felt SO SORRY for the kids who had to watch their mums and dads, and even some grandparents, doing CRINGE-MAKING 80s dancing. Being forced to witness something like that MUST be a form of child abuse. Counsellors should have been available for their POOR kids. For once I was glad that my mum never left the house.

After all the tension of waiting, A&E came on and tuned up. Dean looked fantastic. He had great dress sense – classic jeans, plain black shirt, floppy hair. PERFECT. In the end, I was glad that I hadn't been able to dress up. Wearing jeans (the only pair that still fitted me) and a clean T-shirt gave the message that I wasn't TOO excited about our date, but I'd made an effort to get my hair straight and shiny and put some nice dangly earrings in.

I glanced over to where Ellie and Jen were sitting. Angela was there, too, with a crowd of Goths. She'd dyed her hair black and was wearing a sort of cobwebby T-shirt and a long black skirt. I had to admit that the Goth look quite suited her. Ellie and Jen, on the other hand, looked like they'd been experimenting with a new fake tan. They had orange legs and short white skirts. HIDEOUS. When they looked my way, I made a point of not seeming excited as A&E prepared to play. I tried to sit in a way that said 'I do this all the time, it's almost boring'.

But OH MY GOODNESS! After the first song, I was praying for the floor of the gym to open up and swallow me.

A&E were a COMPLETE DISASTER. I'd heard older kids saying that they'd been fantastic last year, all funky and laid back…and playing their own stuff, no cover versions. How COULD they let me down in my moment of social triumph!

There were problems with the technical bits and pieces. They couldn't hear themselves play. They were all out of synch. The drummer was three beats ahead of the two guitars and the lead singer,

Kat Bell-Wright (known as Kan't Breathe-Right because of her terrible asthma), was obviously a desperate last-minute find. Not one line of the songs came out without her gasping and wheezing. She was raspberry pink by the end of their set and her armpits were bath-sponge-sweaty under her red Lycra top – NEVER a good image if you want to be a Groove Goddess.

I felt SO upset for them and SO EXCRUCIATINGLY EMBARRASSED at the whole thing that I didn't even look in Ellie and Jen's direction at the end, when QT took the prize.

Everyone crowded around the winners so I was able to creep away and slip backstage to where the other bands were packing up. I hovered near the door of the dressing room, which was just the boy's changing room behind the gym, and tried to think of kind things to say to Dean about the performance. I was still having nervous butterflies about meeting him even though the evening wasn't going anything like I'd hoped. OK, so Jen, Ellie and Angela weren't watching, green with envy, as I left with the winner, but Dean was still the best-looking boy in Year Ten, and we still had a date.

I waited a long time. First THE PUSTULES

left, and then PSYCHODELICIOUS, who were grumbling and muttering to one another about how unfair they thought the result had been. When they'd gone I stayed outside the door and could hear Dean and his band arguing. There was quite a bit of shouting and swearing when Dean told Kat Bell-Wright and the others all the things they'd done wrong. Eventually, Dean came out on his own, carrying his guitar, and with a face like a storm cloud.

'Oh, hi. It's you,' he said, looking a bit surprised to see me.

I think he might have forgotten about our date for a moment, because of the argument and the disappointment of losing. That was understandable, I suppose. He must've been feeling awful.

'Are the others coming for pizza?' I asked, but I'd already guessed from all the shouting that they weren't.

'No, they're all a bit depressed,' Dean said. Then he snapped his smile back on. 'I'm starving, though. Shall we go to Gino's?'

So it was just Dean and me having a pepperoni stuffed-crust pizza at ten o'clock.

He was TOTALLY fed up, as you can imagine. He bit hard into the pizza crust and swore through a mouthful of runny cheese, which wasn't very nice to look at, but I forgave him because he was stressed out.

'*Fourth* place!' he said. 'We deserved better than that.'

I didn't think I should say that his band had given a CHRONICALLY AWFUL performance, or that anyone could see they hadn't rehearsed enough, or that the singer sounded like she had chewing gum WEDGED up her nostrils.

Instead, I said what I thought he wanted to hear so that he'd feel better about it.

'You just had a bad night and you were unlucky with the plugs and wires and stuff. All that whistling feedback wasn't your fault.'

Oh dear! I was acting like my mum would've done.

'Yeah, I suppose,' he said. 'And Jess dropping out was a royal pain in the backside.'

He gave me his film star smile again, but I felt like he was just practising it on me. It seemed a bit fake, and it wasn't QUITE so attractive with pizza crumbs between his teeth, but it made me feel more relaxed to see that he was just human, after all. I couldn't help offering a bit of advice DISGUISED AS A QUESTION.

'Will you be keeping the new singer?'

He screwed his nose up.

'Doubt it.'

'Good idea. I thought she was a bit of a *weak link* in the line up.'

He agreed with this, too, and tucked away the last of his pizza a bit more cheerfully.

Dean insisted on paying so I let him because in my favourite films women don't pay for dinner when they get taken out by handsome men. I don't know if it was the RIGHT thing to do, but it made me feel more sophisticated.

We got the same bus home. Dean only lived a few streets from me, but not on the estate. His parents had a big house closer to the old part of town. It had electric gates and they kept two Doberman dogs that walked around the garden at night. Dean lit a cigarette. I didn't mind. It made him look mature, except that I couldn't help noticing that he still had hands like a little boy. I notice things like that because the men in films I watch always have beautiful, square hands. Dean's didn't look like that, but I pretended to myself that they did so that it felt romantic, strolling home with him in the dark.

We walked past the park. I sometimes went through it on my way back from school, if the evenings were light and there were joggers and dog-walkers around.

'We could go this way, if you want,' he suggested, nodding towards the park gates.

'No. Too scary,' I said, rubbing my hands up and down my jumper sleeves.

He slipped his arm around me. 'I'll protect you,' he joked.

I wasn't as nervous and fluttery as I'd expected I would be, and I was just thinking that it felt quite natural and OK having his arm there, when he suddenly stepped in front of me and shoved his mouth on top of mine without any warning and started giving me a SLOPPY, WET, FAGS-AND-PIZZA-SMELLING kiss.

I pushed him off.

'Hey. I didn't say you could do that.'

He gave a short, surprised laugh, like no one had stopped him before and said, 'Didn't know I was supposed to ask.'

'Well, you should, so back off.'

'But I want to kiss you.'

And he tried it again.

And I shoved him off again.

'I'LL decide when I'm kissed, thank you. And who by.'

All the romance fell away with a horrible CL$_A$T$_T$ER and he just looked like any other pushy boy, not like a film star at all, not by a MILLION MILES, and that was NOT GOOD ENOUGH. It wasn't good enough for me AT ALL. A girl who is going to be the *✶✶ **GREATEST** ✦✶✦ **costume designer in the history of cinema** does NOT want her love life to start with a fags and cheesy pizza snog from a boy with undersized hands!

His laugh went a bit spiteful, a bit sideways out of his mouth.

'What makes you so special that you can be fussy?' he said. 'You're just a Year Seven groupie.'

That made me **BOIL**.

'**WHAT!?**'

'You're just a hanger-on.'

My mouth fell open in a gasp.

'How **DARE** you? You **CREEP!** You **INVITED** me.'

He stepped back and looked me up and down, his lip curled up in a sneer, like I was a pile of something nasty on the pavement.

'Only to make up numbers. We can't play to an empty hall.'

I shoved him backwards, **_HARD_**, and he fell into a hedge. Then I ran home, the **_HOTTEST EVER_** tears of shame pouring down my cheeks.

CORDELIA CODD, YOU ARE AN IDIOT!

Mum was in bed. I wanted to wake her, to shake her shoulder and tell her what had happened. I wanted her to tell Dean Frampton's mum what a **_RAT_** her son was. I wanted someone to sort him out, to **_PUNISH_** him. But I couldn't just go and wake her, it wasn't fair when she was poorly and needed so much sleep. And if I told her where I'd been she might throw a STRESSY FIT and be anxious and cross about me telling her I'd been to Drusilla's when I hadn't.

I was on my own with this one. I sat in the kitchen and tried to calm down. I told Mr Belly about it as I fed him extra biscuits from my shaking hand. He rubbed his head on my leg and purred.

'If Dad was here,' I told him through my tearful sniffles, 'he'd have a HARD WORD with Dean's parents. What Dad would call "a bit of a dialogue".'

Dad was good at that. He could lose his temper sometimes, but mostly he just had long conversations with people and sorted things out, like Mum did. Although something like this might just SNAP HIS TETHER and there'd be an ALMIGHTY ROW at Dean's house. I just wanted my dad to stick up for me. I wanted him to come home and make a BIG SCENE. Then Dean would HAVE to apologise, or be grounded by his parents in their posh house, FOR EVER.

In the days when Dad loved me he would've done that.

In the days when he was here to look after us.

Upstairs in my room I tugged the napkin from Gino's out of my pocket and jumped on it, pretending it was Dean's guitar. I still had my shoes on and they left big dusty footprints. Then I lay awake for ages, seriously doubting that I would EVER go out with a boy again.

I thought things were as bad as they could get but, yet again, I was

WRONG WRONG WRONG.

14

Of course, I owed Dru a BIG FAT apology, and I needed someone to tell the whole HORRIBLE Friday night story to. The shame of Battle of the Bands was stuck in my aching head. All through Saturday, I couldn't stop worrying about whether Dru would forgive me and be friends again. Only watching Ava Gardner in *Pandora and the Flying Dutchman* took my mind off it for a while – that film has more beautiful dresses than any other film I've seen IN MY LIFE SO FAR. But even though I made about a zillion drawings in my sketchbook, I couldn't stop thinking how I URGENTLY needed to talk to Dru.

On Sunday I couldn't stand it ANY LONGER.

I had to know if Dru was going to forgive me for being an IDIOT, so I took a BIG BRAVE BREATH and walked round to her house in the afternoon, while Mum was having a nap. I was ABSOLUTELY ready to grovel and admit that she'd been right about Dean. I practised how I was going to say sorry to her over and over in my head as I walked but, when I got there, her house was dark and empty. She was probably out having fun with her lovely family, I thought, which made me feel even more miserable. All I could do was walk back to my grim little house and watch *It's a Wonderful Life*, which is a very good film if you need A GOOD SOB.

Monday morning seemed to take weeks to arrive, not just two days. I finally caught up with Drusilla in the corridor before registration. All I managed to say was, 'I'm sorry, Dru. You were right about Dean. He's a prize creep…' before my voice got stuck in my throat and I burst into tears.

Dru pulled me into an empty classroom.

'Jeez, what happened, Cordelia? You look like a

truck ran over you or something.'

And I spat the whole story out like hot marbles bubbling up through gushes of tears. I told her all the details. She stood with her mouth open, punctuating my story with

'No!'

and *'Eugh!'*

and *'How dare he?'*

and *'What a creepoid!'*

But when I'd finished babbling at her and there was steam coming out my buttonholes, Drusilla couldn't resist. She clicked her tongue and tipped her head to one side. 'I *told* you so.'

My eyes filled up again. 'Thanks a LOT, Dru. That's not very supportive.'

Drusilla winced and touched my arm. It was her turn to apologise.

'Sorry sorry sorry. I'm *so* tactless, sometimes. Anyway…' she flipped a hand. 'He's history…and we're friends again. That's what matters.'

She was right AGAIN.

By the time we got to Double English I was starting to relax about the whole thing. I practised flipping my hand, like Drusilla, and saying to myself,

'He's history…he's history…'

Mr Grimpson had left another giant string of sentences on the board for us to pull apart. He must've left them the night before, knowing that he was going to be delayed getting in. Drusilla joked that he'd probably had to take a time trip back to 1935 to get a new suit. There were instructions about finding 'five million nouns' and 'four trillion adjectives' written underneath, but they were mostly blocked out by half the class crowding around the board, craning their necks to see something that was stuck there. Drusilla and I pushed forward with everyone else to check out what the fuss was about. A sheet of A4 paper with a photo printed on it had been sticky-taped over Mr Grimpson's instructions. As I edged towards it, other kids stopped talking, nudged each other and stepped back. They seemed to be looking at me and then back at the photo. There was a scraping and clattering of chairs as they moved away from the board, tripping and stumbling because they kept their eyes on me. I frowned. This wasn't about who sat next to who. It wasn't about them being scared of me because of the Ellie Treatment. This was something new, something BIG.

Drusilla and I moved closer to the photo.

Her jaw dropped immediately.

My brain took a second to catch up, and then my eyes sprang out so far they nearly hit the board.

'*Jeez*, Cordelia,' Drusilla whispered.

She reached out and tugged the photo down before I had time to react. Despite the shock, she behaved calmly. She could see that I was PARALYSED with horror and said quietly, 'Don't worry.'

Then she squeezed my arm and turned to the class, calling out, 'Any *idiot* can see it's not real.'

I felt myself turn as pale as school custard. My legs were about to give way. Dru shuffled me to a desk and we sat down. I forced myself to take another look at the picture. SOMEONE had taken a photo of me from the school magazine. I remembered the interview. It was my first week of school. An eager reporter from Year Nine had asked, 'How does it feel to be at Beckmere?'

I was smiling, happy to tell him that it 'all seemed great so far'.

SOMEONE had used a computer to stick **THAT** photo of **MY** head onto the body of a **VERY NAKED LADY**. So it looked like me, but with enormous boobs and a big curvy bum. I looked like a circus freak, a **STARK NAKED CIRCUS FREAK**. My breathing started going fast, in and out over my teeth again, and my head thumped.

I stood up. I heard Drusilla say, 'It's OK. Let the teachers deal with it.'

But I couldn't help myself. I stared around the room. Jen and Ellie were looking pleased and catty. Angela was sitting with her new friend, Rozia. Both of them looked down at their desks so that our eyes wouldn't meet. None of them knew much about computers so I didn't think they would have done it. I looked at Stinky Sonya, Richard Antrobus, Martin Hinckley, Andrew Parsimon, Ruby Khan, Ahmed Collins. They all stared back at me, waiting. Waiting to see me DIE of shame and SLIDE through the floor, or evaporate in a green cloud like something from a laboratory.

'Who was it?' I asked, my voice not sounding nearly as angry as I felt.

Apart from Angela and Rozia, Matthew Pilling was one of the few people in the room not looking at me. But he looked up now, with a big grin on his spotty face. I was about to fly across the room and **PULVERISE** him, but he blurted out a question, which stopped me just in time.

'What will you do to whoever it was when

you find out?'

'None of your business…but it will **_HURT_**.'

'Good.' He tapped a rhythm with his ruler on the desk. 'In that case I have pleasure in telling you,' he waved the ruler around the room, 'and everyone here was a witness, that it was Dean Frampton. He stuck it there about ten minutes before you arrived.'

Matthew was the drummer in one of the other school bands. They'd been knocked out of Battle of the Bands by A&E at the semifinals. He'd never liked Dean.

OF COURSE!

It was SO OBVIOUS.

I wouldn't let Dean snog me so he'd got his NASTY LITTLE REVENGE by doing this. My mouth was filling up with the worst names I could think of, but I zipped them in. They needed to hit the right target, and I knew just where to find him.

Drusilla tried to stop me. She grabbed at my sleeve, but I was out the door too fast for her.

'Hang on. We've got witnesses,' she called after me. 'He'll get suspended at the very least!'

But I was off down the corridor.

I heard the class tripping over one another and over the desks and chairs to come and see what I was going to do. I passed Mr Grimpson's big tweed-suited body as I ran.

He boomed after me in his rolling voice, like a thundercloud. 'No *rrrunning*, Miss Codd! And my English class is in *this* direction…' He pointed a chubby finger towards the classroom, but his voice tailed off when he saw the rest of the class hanging out of the room, staring after me.

'And *you lot* had better have the exercise on the *board* complete by the time I have my *books* out of my *briefcase*… I'll deal with Miss Codd later,' I heard him bellow.

I was already halfway to the gym. I knew EXACTLY what I was going to do.

I'd seen just the thing I needed hanging up in the storeroom at the back of the sports hall. I'd noticed all kinds of other stuff in there when we'd had to lug equipment out of the cupboard for gymnastics – some of it for us, some of it for the adult classes that went on in the evening. My weapon was somewhere behind the aerobics steps and the plastic weights, next to the yoga mats. From down the corridor I could see that the hall was open, and I could hear a basketball bouncing around inside.

I peeked in.

Year Nine were having games.

I sneaked up to the open cupboard. No one bothered about me, a little Year Seven kid. The teacher was busy telling someone off for spitting on the wooden floor. From inside the cupboard, surrounded by its rubbery smells, I heard her shout, 'Would you do that on the floor at home!?'

'No, miss.'

'Then don't do it here! Get a paper towel *IMMEDIATELY*!'

I grabbed my weapon and ran for the staircase that led to the top corridor where Year Ten boys hung out a lot, mostly because the drinks machines were better up there. The stairs were narrow and smelled of disinfectant, wood, dried-up chewing gum and the burst insides of ink pens. At the top there was a big, round light in the ceiling and a door with a glass panel. I peeked through as I shoved the bright red boxing glove onto my right hand. Inside it I flexed my fingers to get them comfortable.

Peering through the glass more carefully, I scanned the corridor. There were about a dozen boys hanging out there, probably waiting to be let into a classroom. Dean was standing by the drinks machine, talking and laughing over his shoulder with two friends, who were sitting on the wide window ledge behind him. He was struggling to get the drink he wanted, thumping the side of the machine and poking his fingers in the change tray. His two friends already had their drinks; the cans were next to them on the window ledge, along with a **WHOLE PILE** of white A4 paper that looked like more copies of the **HORRIBLE** photo. He was obviously intending to stick them up **EVERYWHERE**.

My breathing jumped in and out, and the inside of my head was like drums thudding. I pushed the door open quietly and walked up the corridor until I was right beside Dean. Before he had time to look up and notice me, I swung a right hook at the back of his head with the boxing glove.

WHAT A PUNCH!

I was amazed at how strong I was. That punch had all my **RAGING** behind it. Dean's forehead bounced off the drinks machine, leaving a big dent in the picture of bubbles on its metal front. He looked at me, his eyes not quite focused, and before he had time to realise what had happened, I swung a second ALMIGHTY punch that got him on the bottom lip and knocked him backwards. One of his feet, in its expensive trainer, went into a waste paper basket full of leftover sandwiches and drink cans. He toppled, knocking his friends and their drinks flying. They just GAWPED, their mouths dangling like dribbly bloodhounds as I scooped up the photos and left. Tears were pushing up through me and they were about to spill out, so I had to clear off before Dean saw them. I just had time to shout, 'You won't be kissing anyone for a while, now…**YOU COMPLETE CREEPY TOTAL UTTER LOSER!**' Then I grabbed the pile of photos and ran for the door, pausing for a microsecond to shout back, 'And your band is **A PILE OF CRAP!**' before flying down the stairs as if some HORROR-ZOMBIE version of Mr Grimpson was chasing me.

I backtracked to the gym. The Year Nine basketball match was well underway so I was able to creep in and hang the glove up just where I'd found it without anyone noticing me. Then I ducked into the changing rooms and out through the back entrance, near the dustbins.

I stood, tearing the photos into shreds and feeding them in under the big plastic flap at the front of the paper-recycling bin. It was hard to see what I was doing through my fuzzy tears. Then I went back to English, only stopping in the changing rooms for a minute to wash my face and hands. I was ready to explain myself to Mr Grimpson, ready to admit to everything I'd just done – but underneath I was still angry, not just because of what Dean had done, but because I had no mum or dad here to come and sort it out for me.

15

Dean was suspended when it all came out. He wasn't allowed back into school until after the half-term holidays, at the beginning of June. Drusilla had kept the copy of the photo from the white board as evidence. Smart thinking. I had to be interviewed by the head, Mrs Greenlaw, but I said I would only go to her office if Dru was with me and if Dean was NOT in the same room.

They were fine about that, but Mrs Greenlaw said she would have to write to my parents because of the seriousness of the incident. I BEGGED her not to and explained about Dad not being there any more and Mum being broken-hearted and poorly and stressed and how she wouldn't cope with it AT

ALL and how I could handle it fine with the help of the teachers, because they were SO kind and supportive. I had to say that last bit because I was DESPERATE for her not to send a letter. Then she suggested writing to Dad instead and it all came out about him not caring anyway or he would never have left us and that made Mrs Greenlaw frown and look a bit worried, like I was a problem.

She gave me a 'talking to' about being out of class, stealing school equipment and using violence, but she didn't write a letter to Mum or Dad. The week after, I had to go to a special 'session' with a counsellor, a thin lady who wore black-rimmed glasses and expensive-looking shoes.

According to Dru, talking to counsellors is something Americans do all the time and it can be quite useful if you think you're a little bit mad but not quite 'off your trolley'. I thought it would be stupid and embarrassing, but it turned out to be OK. It gave me a chance to spill my moans to a complete stranger, someone who would listen while I prattled on about Mum and Dad and all the stuff I had to do at home, and Ellie's bogey and Dean's RAT STINK behaviour. She let me have a good rant and feel a bit sorry for myself. After all, Mum was pretty much out of action in the listening-to-your-child's-problems department at the moment so it was the first chance I'd had for a good long moan to an adult in ages.

The counsellor nodded a lot and said kind things, and was sympathetic, and I did cry a bit and felt less angry afterwards, but it didn't bring my dad back, did it? It didn't make Dean Frampton **BURST INTO FLAMES AND DIE**. It didn't make Miss Haliborn like me, or Mr Grimpson let me off all the homework I'd not done, or make my mum 'normal' again.

Drusilla and I went for lunch in the canteen after the session with the counsellor. Thankfully, there was chocolate pudding on offer that day. It was a NEED CHOCOLATE PUDDING DAY if ever there was one.

On our way back to lessons Drusilla made a suggestion that terrified me.

'Maybe I should come to your place and help out a bit with some of the jobs you have to do.'

I FROZE. I couldn't let anyone come to our house. Maggie didn't have time to help Mum as much as she wanted to and, although I was doing what I could, it was a rubbish tip. It smelled bad, even though I'd tried really hard to find out what had got stuck behind the fridge and gone mouldy. The living-room curtains were hanging off and the kitchen floor was sticky. I'd DIE of embarrassment if Dru found out how DEEPLY GRIM things were at my house. The vacuum cleaner made a DEAD DOG stink and I didn't know how to get Mr Belly's hairs off the cushion covers. I blushed and said, 'No. I… My mum gets nervous about visitors.'

We were already late for Science. Drusilla just shrugged as we scurried along. 'OK.'

Then she frowned.

'Doesn't *anyone* help you? I mean, if my mother was a *loony toon,* I'd get help.'

I stopped walking. She saw me go red and breathe in sharply.

HOW DARE SHE CALL MY MUM THAT!

The cleaner's cupboard was just behind Dru. My first thought was to shove her in there and do something **BRUTAL** to her with a bucket. She must've realised because she clutched both hands over her mouth like the words had just come out by accident.

'Jeez, I'm sorry, Cordelia. I didn't mean…'

'My mum is **NOT** a loony. My dad left us and she's worn out and sad, OK?'

'OK. I'm *really* sorry. Sometimes I'm *so* clumsy

with the words I use.'

'Mum's tired. She's just tired, and upset because of Dad. You're lucky I don't snap your glasses, y'know.'

I hitched my school bag further onto my shoulder and we walked on. Drusilla could be as blunt as a haddock's head some days. Considering how brainy she was, she could be so STUPID about little things – little things that made people want to hit her or shove her into cupboards. She walked beside me, but only stayed quiet for a moment before she asked, 'Have you heard from your dad lately? Is he still in London?'

I curled my lip up in a DON'T-KNOW-DON'T-CARE sort of way.

'I think so.'

'Does he write to you?'

'Once, ages ago. I tore the letter up, though.'

Drusilla pointed to the toilets. She always had to wee after lunch for some reason. So we headed in there, even though we were late. She called to me from inside the cubicle.

'He sounds irresponsible. He should come back and help.'

'I know. But I can't MAKE him, can I?'

Dru flushed the loo and came out to wash her hands.

'You could try. He should at least know that your mom is having a hard time. And so are you.'

That made me wonder. Did Dad KNOW how poorly Mum was?

By the end of the day we'd decided that getting Dad back was the ONLY real solution to my problems, as long as he came back determined to be a BETTER Dad and a MUCH better husband to Mum. He just HAD to come home so that he could help with Mum and stick up for me and just generally BE THERE and do Dad stuff.

This was something I was going to HAVE to do, with Drusilla's help. I had to take responsibility for getting my parents back together. Teachers and counsellors and other grown-ups couldn't be relied on. They would UNDOUBTEDLY mess it up.

Drusilla said she'd back me ALL THE WAY. So we set about making a plan. At first I thought our idea was just a dream, the sort of thing I would've LIKED to be able to do. But then something happened to make me realise that it was REAL, and that I actually HAD to carry out the BONKERS plan we came up with.

16

Usually Mum was asleep, wrapped up in her pink fleece blanket on the sofa, when I got home. But she wasn't there that afternoon and when I went upstairs to check on her, she wasn't in bed, either. I came back down to the kitchen and as I opened the door I knocked the rubbish bin by accident. The noise startled something that was under the table. At first I thought it must be Mr Belly. Sometimes he gets into a fight and then sits under the table, licking his wounds. But when I bent down to look it wasn't Mr Belly, it was Mum. My heart thumped and I felt sick because I thought that something really bad must've happened.

'Mum?'

I looked around the kitchen quickly in case there'd been a burglary or someone was outside the window. My heartbeats were so frantic that they stuck in my windpipe and made me pant. Bending down further so that I could see her better, I tried to talk calmly, as if I wasn't afraid.

'What's wrong, Mum? What's happened? What are you doing down there?'

Her hands were clasped tight over her ears and her face was down low, near the sticky floor.

'Nothing's wrong,' she said. 'I just don't want to come out. I can't. It's noisy.'

'It's just the radio. Shall I turn it off?'

'Yes, please.'

The radio always sat next to the toaster. I switched it off but kept looking towards Mum, curled up in her dressing gown, scared stiff of something. I started to reach into my blazer pocket for my mobile.

'Mum. I don't think you're very well. I'm going to call Dr Khan.'

That seemed to make her panic more.

'No. No. I just want to stay here.'

My hands were shaking. My mum had REALLY dropped her basket this time. Dru's number was the first to come up.

'Mum, *I* need some help. You're not being normal and I can't cope with it.'

She was shuffling further under the table. What was going on in her head?

'Mum, you're scaring me.'

'It's OK. I just can't come out.'

I backed out of the kitchen and called Dru. She would know what to do. Her phone seemed to ring for ages before she answered, all perky and calm, as usual.

My voice went crackly as I tried not to cry.

'Dru…?'

'Cordelia? You sound weird. What's up?'

I could only just get the words out.

'My mum's under the kitchen table and she won't come out. I need help…'

I heard Dru take one short breath in. That was probably all the time it took her super-sensible brain to decide what was best.

'OK. Stay put. And don't worry. My aunt Bethany used to do this all the time. It's probably just a panic attack. We'll be there in *five* minutes. Call your doctor.'

'She says not to.'

'Sounds like she doesn't know what's best just now. Call him. We're on our way.'

I took a deep breath and dialled Dr Khan's number. It was kept on the pin board in the kitchen where we stuck postcards and takeaway menus. When it started ringing, I went out into the hall again and closed the kitchen door so Mum wouldn't hear. Zillions of TERRIBLE ideas scrambled round in my head. What if my mum got taken away to a special hospital? What then?

What would they do to her?

What would happen to me?

What would happen to Mr Belly?

The receptionist put me through to Dr Khan straight away. He said he'd be here as soon as possible. Then I went slowly back into the kitchen and crouched down with my back against the kitchen cupboards. Washing-up was piled above me around the sink. The sticky, dirty floor was littered with cat biscuits again. Dru was going to find out what a mess we lived in. It was all going to be terrible and humiliating, but there was nothing I could do about that now – Mum was the most important thing at the moment.

I waited and waited for what seemed like

hours, but was probably less than ten minutes, sitting on the floor with my back against the kitchen cupboards, watching my mum being bonkers under the table. Mum didn't speak. I didn't speak. There was just the sound of Mr Belly crunching cat biscuits to break the scary silence.

Dru and Jess didn't ring the bell when they arrived. One of them knocked gently and then they came straight in. I looked at Mum, then at Dru, and then I burst into BLUBBING because Dru and Jess looked so sunny and beautiful when they came in and my WHOLE LIFE felt like such an UGLY MESS.

My shaky voice said, 'My mum's not well, Dru.'

Dru and Jess glanced around the kitchen. They MUST have been shocked at the state of it, but they didn't say anything. Jess bent down and introduced herself to Mum then chatted to her gently. Dru whispered to me.

'You know what?'

'I know. You were right. My mum's a loony, isn't she?'

Dru fished a paper hanky out of her pocket and handed it to me.

'No! Nothing *like*. My aunt and my mum both

did this last year. Mum locked herself in the bathroom for two days and Dad had to feed her through the window. She's fine now.'

'Really?'

'Yeah, really.'

'They didn't take her away?'

She flipped a hand saying, 'Nah. Don't worry. It was pretty scary at the time, though.'

Just then I had a RANDOM ★ FILM ★ MOMENT ★ . Something popped into my head. I knew Dru would understand.

'I feel like I've got the Mean Reds, like in *Breakfast at Tiffany's*, when Audrey Hepburn says, "Sometimes you're afraid and you don't know what you're afraid of".'

Dru nodded and smiled.

'Except,' I said, still whispering so as not to give Mum the JIBBERING JUMPIES, 'except that now I think I know what I'm afraid of. You know all that really annoying stuff that parents do, like the way they go on about clean clothes and vacuuming and eating vegetables and fruit and tidying your room?'

'Yeah, don't I just,' said Dru.

'Well, we hate all that nagging because it's a PAIN IN THE BACKSIDE, but when no one is saying those things, when no one is doing all that fussing and your house just gets left in a big smelly mess, now THAT'S scary. I don't know how to keep things organised for myself and I'm angry that no one is doing it for me, like mums and dads should do. It's as if all the safe, warm, clean things around me have disappeared and I'm left with a stinky cat tray and a bin covered in flies and no one reminding me when to use a clean towel.'

'Maybe that's why you got angry and stuck a bag over Ellie's head,' said Dru. 'I guess being angry and being afraid can get mixed up sometimes, and then you have no patience left when people do annoying stuff. Maybe that's what happens when you get the *Mean Reds*.'

We both nodded, like we'd solved a big mystery, which we had. It sounds obvious now, but sometimes REALLY obvious things, things that are right on the end of our noses, can be the hardest to see.

By bedtime that night Mum was calmer. I think the doctor gave her some new medicine. He spoke to Jess, as she was the oldest. Later, she and Dru brought their mum round to help out. I was told to go to school as usual the next day and that Dru's mum and Jess would come around in the morning to be with Mum.

I didn't want to leave Mum and go to school, but I did. When I came home the house was tidy and clean. It was SO lovely to see our house fresh and shiny again. Mum was dressed and having a cup of tea with Dru's mum, and Maggie was there, too. As I kicked off my shoes in the little hallway I heard Maggie talking about something to do with the office. Mr Snaul was mentioned, but I couldn't catch what it was about. When I came in they stopped talking seriously and acted a bit jollier. I noticed some official-looking papers on the table, but I didn't pay much attention to them because I was so pleased that Mum had other ladies there.

Just having friends round wasn't going to fix things properly though, was it? It was a bit like putting sticky tape over a hole in the road – it wasn't going to solve the problem for long. So I knew for certain that the plan I'd worked out with Dru, even if it was COMPLETELY WACKO, HAD to be put into action, IMMEDIATELY.

17

This is the time to grab hold of my GRIM
SITUATION and MAKE it change – TONIGHT
is the night that Dru and I HAVE to make the plan
work. It's been just over a week since Mum's panic
attack. She's recovered, but she still hasn't been out
much, except with Maggie for a cup of coffee. At
least she's been getting up and dressed most days.
But things are still nowhere near back to normal.
And, although it's REALLY kind of Dru's mum and
Maggie to keep popping round to check on Mum
and help tidy up a bit, we can't expect them to sort
out our home as well as their own, can we?

It's already late June. My first year at Beckmere
will soon be over and Dru and I have decided that

the term MUST have a happy ending.

Dru is panting with excitement. 'Quick, upstairs, I've got something for you.'

I've been invited to sleep over at Dru's for Friday and Saturday night. Mum said she intends to snooze on the sofa for most of the weekend so I don't need to worry about her. But I did the laundry and hung it up to dry after school, made lots of tuna mayonnaise, and bought extra bread, cheese and milk from the corner shop so that I can be sure she'll have some food and won't have to think about housework while I'm gone. Then I stuffed a change of clothes and my toothbrush into a backpack, said goodbye, and sprinted round to Dru's as fast as I could.

Dru springs up the stairs ahead of me. I glance into the kitchen and wave to Jess, who has headphones on. She raises a hand to signal hello and wiggles her fingers, then goes back to painting her nails.

'Mom and Dad are away visiting my aunt Zillah this weekend,' says Dru, 'and Jess is going out, so it's *perfect*. Here.'

She hands me an envelope and then tucks her hands in the back pockets of her jeans, grinning. I put down my backpack and tear into the envelope. Inside are two long, thin bus tickets – outward and return – to London. The bus to London leaves in two hours. I gasp.

'When did you get these?'

'I went to the booking office straight from school.'

'I'm really doing this, aren't I? I'm not dreaming?'

Dru shakes her head.

'No changing your mind now. It's a present, so it'd be rude to chicken out.'

She's smiling – a huge grin – and her big eyes are twinkling with excitement. I check the tickets again. They cost twice what I have in my pocket. I hug her – our first hug – and say 'thank you' over and over. Then I'm suddenly SO scared.

'What shall I say to him when I get there?'

Dru looked surprised.

'To your dad?'

'Yes. I don't want to go all that way to just blub in front of him and get angry.'

She gives her usual shrug and says, 'Why not?'

'Because I'm going there to get him back. I need to be GROWN UP and EXPLAIN things.'

We sit down, Dru on her computer chair and me on the edge of her bed.

'So what if you *do* get upset at first? It's OK. If I hadn't seen my dad in that long, I'd be *howling*. If you can't *blah* in front of your own dad, where can you do it?'

I turn the tickets over in my hands and stare at them. The next twenty-four hours could be the most CRUCIAL of my entire life so far. I want to get them right.

'I've never seen you cry, Dru. Do you?'

She raises her arms up and looks at the ceiling.

'Do we *cry* in this family? Boy, YES. We *blub* and **SHOUT** and *sulk* and **STORM ABOUT**, then my aunt Zillah usually comes round. She bursts in with her arms open…and you don't argue with those arms, they're, like, *this* big.' Dru puts her hands out in front to show the width, about as fat as a FAT DOG'S MIDDLE. I laugh at the idea, and then Dru stands up and acts out being her aunt Zillah.

'She throws her arms out like this…and yells in her German accent. Vot are you doing to mine heartz viz dis fighting I am hearing about? You, who I love zo much. I skveez you all like leetle lemons if you doesn't shtop it.'

She sits down again.

'Then we all *laugh* and *cry* some more and *hug*

and cook an *enormous* dinner.'

I've never seen Dru so funny. Maybe we're both a bit MANIC with excitement about THE PLAN because we roll around holding our stomachs, giggling like drains until Dru suddenly stops, her eyes wide open.

'We need to get down to business. Let's find a map. Got the address?'

I nod and pull the scraps of Dad's letter out of the front pocket of my backpack.

Dru screws her nose up.

'What happened to that?'

'I told you. I tore it up. I was cross. It's been under my bed for months.'

'Jeez. I hope you never get *that* cross with *me*. Look at the *state* of it. Never mind, we just need a postcode.'

Her fingers skitter over the keyboard like clever little mouse feet.

CLICK, CLICK,
          TAP~PET~Y, TAP~PET~Y,
                    CLICK, CLICK.

A map site comes up on the internet. Meanwhile, I rummage through the pieces of Dad's letter for the address, laying them out on her bedspread

'Aha!' I shout at last, holding up a tiny fragment of paper. Dru squints at it, then turns and types in the postcode. In less than a minute the printer is chugging out a map of the roads around my dad's address, with the nearest Underground station marked on it. Dru runs downstairs while I study the print out. Does Dad live on a busy street, I wonder, with buses and ambulances going by all night? Or a quiet one, like ours, with just lawn mowers and birds singing? You can't tell much from a road map; it doesn't have smells and noise.

Dru comes back with a plan of the London Underground, which she spreads out on the bed. We set about tracking the best route from Victoria Station, where I'll arrive at eleven o'clock tonight, through to the station nearest to my dad's place in North London. Following the squiggly lines of the train routes with her finger, Dru scribbles down directions for me on a sheet of paper.

'I've been to London a few times. It's easy to get around on the tube.'

She writes the directions down and I can't help wondering why I'VE never been to London. There must be SO much to see. I make a note in my head to ask Dad to show me around properly – once he's agreed to come home, that is – and has bought his ticket so that I know he means it.

Dru shoves the top back on her pen.

'Done. We're ready. All we have to do is wait for Jess to go out. We've got plenty of time before the bus leaves.'

I look at the maps over and over again. The street map and the Underground plan look complicated to me. I ask lots of ANXIOUS PANTS questions.

'When will your mum and dad get back?'

'Not until Sunday night. We don't have to worry about them. And Jess won't wake up until after midday tomorrow. By then I'll have left her a note saying we've had breakfast and have gone to look around the shops in town.'

'But what about Saturday evening? Isn't Jess supposed to be "in charge" and cooking dinner and everything?'

'I've covered that one. I'll tell her that you decided that one night was long enough to leave your mom on her own, so you went home. She won't question it.'

GENIUS. Sneaky but BRILLIANT.

So why am I feeling so WIMPISH?

'I have to top up my phone,' I say.

'We can do that at the bus station,' says Dru. 'There's a newsagent's there. Have you got your dad's number?'

'Yes, it's on my phone.'

Then Dru is very strict with me. 'Remember, *don't* call him until you get out of the tube station near his house, even if you're feeling scared. If you call him from the bus to let him know you're arriving he might come and meet you and send you straight home again.'

'OK. I promise.'

My arrival at Dad's place had to be a COMPLETE surprise. That way there'd be no time for PARENTAL ALERTS. I couldn't have Dad calling Mum and letting her know that I'd put myself on a bus to London. She would stress herself right back under the kitchen table and Dad would have the police hunting me down before I could say MISSION ACCOMPLISHED.

Then Jess calls, 'Bye, you two,' from downstairs. We rush to the landing and hang over the banister.

'Bye,' we both call.

'Have a good time, sis,' Dru adds. 'What time'll you be back?'

Jess smiles up at us and wags a finger tipped with lovely purple nail polish.

'*Way* after you two are asleep, *got that*?'

Dru waves a DVD in the air.

'We're gonna watch movies and raid the fridge.'

Jess checks her lipstick in the hall mirror.

'Sounds like a good plan. I'll cook dinner for us all tomorrow.'

'Great!' we chirp, like a pair of budgies.

She leaves, looking FABULOUS in a green floaty top and tatty jeans.

I feel SLIGHTLY guilty about telling her a lie, but some things are just TOO IMPORTANT for people 'in charge' to know about. They'd mess it all up for us, wouldn't they?

By eight o'clock we're at the bus station. Dru gives me a final check over before departure.

'OK. You've got the tickets, maps, and some money for the Underground.'

I nod.

'We topped your phone up.'

I keep nodding.

'You have a drink and a sandwich, and something to read.'

Nod, nod, nod. I hold up my copy of *Stars and Screen* magazine. Then we have one last hug.

'And as soon as you get to London you text me, OK?'

'I promise.'

'And text me again when you get out of the tube station.'

'Yes.'

'And again when you've called your dad.'

'Yep.'

'And again as soon as you get to his apartment.'

'Yep. Phew! I hope you never join the army or some secret terrorist gang, Dru. You'd be SO organised the enemy wouldn't stand a chance.'

'…because if you don't text me,' she goes on, ignoring me, 'I will DIE of *anxious anticipatory angina*.'

'What's that?'

'It's like *worry-and-suspense-causing-my-heart-to-stop*.'

'Nothing serious, then,' I say, smiling.

We have ANOTHER last-minute hug. We're both terrified and excited and CERTAIN that what we're doing is the right thing for everyone – ABSOLUTELY CERTAIN, underneath all the scariness.

So how can we POSSIBLY fail?

18

The lady sitting next to me on the bus is wearing a beautiful pink, beaded sari, but that doesn't excuse the window-rattling snores that are GRUNTLING up from inside her nasal passages. It's INCREDIBLE that some people can just nod off like that and not hear themselves.

I will NEVER snore and I will never MARRY anyone who snores.

I peer out of the window for quite a long time, looking into the cars that whiz past us and wondering if the people in them are going to homes full of big funny relatives like Dru's aunt Zillah.

Dru is SO lucky. Her family is like a bright, bouncy cushion. It's weird to think that I used to

look down my stuck-up nose at her. Now I'm green,
yellow and livid lime with ENVY. I'd swap anything
– my films, my best pastel sticks, my favourite
snuggle blanket, my oldest, dearest soft, squishy toy,
Mr Dog, who's in my backpack – but that's a secret
because, most of the time, I'm WAY too mature
and sophisticated for soft toys. I would even give
up my dream of being **the ✦✦ GREATEST ✦✦**
costume designer in the history of
cinema for a family like Dru has. Not that I want
a DIFFERENT family. I want the same mum and
dad, but with the fun and cosiness put back in.

We're in the city now. Shops, offices and blocks
of flats tower over the bus. The last of the daylight
is catching their windows. It's almost the longest
day of the year and even at this time of night there
is a little bit of light in the sky. But when I crane
my neck to look above the rooftops, I can see
thunderclouds hanging there, waiting to burst.

Suddenly I remember something. Why am I
thinking of this NOW, when it's too late? There's
something Dru and I forgot. What about THE
EVIL JANET? What about HER, the woman my
dad is supposed to love more than me and Mum,
the one who dragged him off to London? What

if she BLOWS the whole plan? What if she stops me fetching my dad back home? My heart has just dropped into my socks. I knew the plan was BONKERS. I should've known we'd miss one VITAL ingredient. THE EVIL JANET could stop me taking Dad home JUST LIKE THAT, with a SNAP of her witchy fingers. If she's there, what will I say to her? The thought of having to exchange polite 'hellos' makes my throat dry up with DISGUST. I just COULDN'T do it. WHY hadn't we put something into the plan to stop her getting in the way of things?

NATURALLY, I start planning her murder. London is full of railway lines, I've heard. If she got pushed ACCIDENTALLY under a train she'd be UTTERLY MINCED. And I've read somewhere that if you drop electrical equipment into the bath, like a lamp or a hairdryer, when it's plugged in, it's almost ALWAYS fatal. But then there's the difficult bit, getting rid of the body. What would be best? Burying her in the woods? Dumping her in the river or on a rubbish tip? Perhaps Dad will be so convinced of the AWFULNESS he's caused by leaving us that he'll WILLINGLY help me to murder his girlfriend and dump her lifeless body.

All the ideas I come up with seem riddled with problems. The bloodstains, the heavy body bumping down the stairs, disturbing the neighbours, Dad not having a car to use for driving us out of town with a dead woman in the boot, the difficulty of reaching a river or rubbish tip or dense wood without being noticed. Murder is probably messy and very hard to get away with, and we'd NEVER get it all done in time for me to get my return bus and be back in school on Monday. It might be easier to persuade Dad that Mum and I are QUITE SIMPLY MORE IMPORTANT than THE EVIL JANET so that he will instantly DUMP her. This would save us the bother of having to kill her and we wouldn't have to worry about being caught and sent to prison for a million years.

Maybe I'll be lucky and THE EVIL JANET will be away for the weekend. As long as I get time alone with Dad so that we can talk a lot – that's the main thing.

Having given up the idea of murder as too complicated, I begin to think up other ways to wreck their relationship. If THE EVIL JANET is there and insists on trying to be nice to me then I'll have to be TOTALLY OBNOXIOUS. I'll fill her handbags with cornflakes and put glue on her hairbrush. I'll cut the buttons off her blouses and pour jam in her shoes.

I'm enjoying thinking about all the WELL-DESERVED HORRIDNESS that I could do when the driver shouts, 'London, Victoria,' and I suddenly feel small and scared again.

It's dark now and raining heavily. Victoria bus station is like a huge, crowded aircraft hangar. Exhaust fumes make me screw up my eyes and cough. Headlights are glaring and horns are beeping to warn people as the buses and coaches reverse. Old and young people of every size and colour sit waiting or talking loudly over the din of engines and the drumming of the rain bouncing off the metal roof. Everyone is surrounded by luggage. No one seems to be smiling or joking and I can't help wondering where all the glamorous, lively people are, the people I imagined London would be full of. The ordinariness of everything is very disappointing.

Groups of friends and relatives stare up at screens that tell the times of the buses. Bright green letters spell out the destinations.

23.35	Manchester	Cancelled
23.40	Newcastle	Delayed
23.45	Birmingham	On Time
23.55	Aberdeen	Delayed

I move towards the streetlights that I can see at the other side of the station. Mostly, I'm just going along with the flow of people and hoping that this is the way out. I'm doing my best NOT to trip over suitcases being wheeled behind people, or trolleys pushed in front, or buggies with slumped babies sucking dummies. It's as if everyone who lives here has been told to LEAVE TOWN IMMEDIATELY and everyone who lives somewhere else has just arrived to take their places. I spot what looks like the only spare seat IN THE UNIVERSE, and sit down to text Drusilla.

Arrivd fne. On wy 2 Undrgrnd. x

Options
Send
Search

I scroll past some of my EX-friends.

Angie…Bella…Craig…

I wonder where they are and what they're doing

and guess that they won't be doing anything as adventurous as I am right now. I keep scrolling until I come to…

Drusilla

Select

Her number comes up

OK

Sending Message

Peep!

Message sent

I spot a sign for the Underground, tuck my phone away in my backpack and move off in that direction. The signs are easy to follow but it feels like MILES to the Underground station along a big road jam-packed with traffic, even this late at night. Eventually, the signs send me inside another huge station. Dru and I hadn't worked out that **VICTORIA UNDERGROUND STATION** was such a long walk from **VICTORIA BUS STATION**.

This station is brightly lit and jangles with the noise of a voice coming over a speaker every few seconds that sounds like someone shouting into a bucket. I cross the huge, white, polished floor and head down what feels like a MILLION steps into the heat and WHIFFS of dirty dust and old, old air. POOHEY! So this is the London Underground.

'Single to Camden Town, please,' I tell the man inside the ticket booth.

He doesn't look at me, or speak to me. He's having a conversation with a friend sitting behind him, talking about how good his new television is and what he's been watching. He just slings my change and an orange cardboard ticket into the metal dish under his window. I scoop them out then stand staring at a big map on the wall, trying to remember which of the coloured squiggly lines I should follow.

I dig into my bag and pull out Drusilla's instructions.

- *Take the Victoria Line (the light blue one) northbound for 3 stops.*
- *Get off at Warren Street and change to the Northern Line (the black one).*
- *Travel northbound for 3 stops. This is Camden Town. Get out here.*

After watching people go through the barrier for a couple of minutes I understand what I'm supposed to do with my ticket. It goes into a slot and gets whizzed through some MYSTERIOUS PROCESS inside that takes 0.2 of a second, and then POPS out of another slot. You grab it and the little doors open to let you through. Then you stare straight ahead and MARCH.

Why is everyone, and I mean EVERYONE, even little old men no higher than my shoulder with walking sticks, moving so FLIPPING FAST? I try to keep up with the crowd so I don't get trampled. The only relaxed people are a few drunk-looking trampy types who've fallen asleep in the corridors.

I keep checking the signs above my head, chanting, '**VICTORIA LINE**, **NORTHBOUND**, **VICTORIA LINE**, **NORTHBOUND**,' and following the arrows. They lead down HUGE escalators with video screens on the walls advertising theatre shows and dentists and helplines and bank loans and perfume and books and films and my brain feels BOMBARDED with all this information that I don't really need. I just focus on '**VICTORIA LINE**, **NORTHBOUND**, **VICTORIA LINE**, **NORTHBOUND**' until I come to a platform that's SCARILY close to the edge of the track. It says **MIND THE GAP** in big letters on the floor and there's a fat yellow line that you have to stand behind.

On the wall opposite, a huge poster advertises a film with Brad Pitt, who isn't one of my favourite actors, and Julianne Moore, who is FAB and has a face that looks like she's so broken-hearted all the time, a bit like my mum but with blonde hair and a different nose.

Mum!

I feel a sudden, terrible PANG of guilt that I haven't thought about her for HOURS. Is she OK? She'll be fast asleep at this time. I don't have to worry yet, not unless she's forgotten to feed Mr Belly. If she has he'll be causing havoc with the Cat Crunch box and biscuits will be all over the kitchen floor again. Oh dear! But there's no use worrying now. I HAVE to get on with the plan. I HAVE to bring my dad home.

An ALMIGHTY sucking sound suddenly fills the platform. I flatten myself against the wall behind me. Then I straighten up and glance side to side, hoping no one has noticed what an uncool thing I've just done, jumping out of my skin at the sound of a train. Well, it's a pretty scary sound when you haven't heard it before. The train stops and the doors open, like doors in the side of a big silver worm. People almost fall out, it's SO crowded, and the rest of us pile in.

I'm lucky to get a seat, and I can just see the map that's on the wall above the heads of the passengers opposite. Across from me, an old man with long, grey dreadlocks is dozing, his chin resting on his chest and his eyelids opening and closing with the sway of the train as it

CH...CH...CH...UTTLES

through the pitch-dark. Next to him, two girls about the same age as Jess are giggling and talking very fast in Italian. I think it's Italian because it sounds a bit different, but not TOTALLY different from the man beside me, who is arguing LOUDLY with his girlfriend in what is DEFINITELY French.

As we reach the third stop, a recording of a lady's voice says, ever so politely,

'THE...NEXT...STOP...IS...WARREN...STREET... CHANGE...HERE...FOR...THE...NORTHERN...LINE... PLEASE...TAKE...ALL...YOUR...BELONGINGS... WITH...YOU.'

I step onto a platform that looks just like the one I got on at. A black sign with yellow writing shows the **WAY OUT** and another says **NORTHERN LINE**.

This time, the train comes straight away.

It's almost empty. There's just me and a few old ladies. I can't help wondering what old ladies do here that keeps them out at this time of night. Maybe they're being 'fine old gadabouts' like Auntie Deirdre.

Inside the carriage, an oblong screen with scrolling orange writing tells me,

```
THE NEXT STOP IS EUSTON. CHANGE HERE
FOR THE PICCADILLY LINE. PLEASE TAKE
      ALL YOUR BELONGINGS WITH YOU.
```

I watch the same words go round and round until we pull into the station. Two men get on. They smell of beer. Their voices are loud and they have red, sweaty faces. They're speaking English, so I understand what they're saying, but I don't know why they're laughing because their jokes sound PATHETIC to me. Perhaps things seem funnier when you're drunk. They look like complete IDIOTS and are having trouble standing up.

Not very attractive.

An old lady gets on when the men get off. She's wearing a dirty white dress and has about a million carrier bags with her that look like they're stuffed full of other carrier bags. She leans forward in her seat, which is close to mine, and grips the bags tightly, as if they are full of expensive shopping. Her fingernails are long and yellow, like those a witch might have. Her ENORMOUS, wobbly body fills the carriage with a strong smell of wee and sweat, and her wild hair makes her look as MAD as a badger on a windy day. I know she probably can't help being like that, but I'm SO relieved when the lady's voice comes on again and says,

'THE...NEXT...STOP...IS...CAMDEN...TOWN... PLEASE...TAKE...ALL...YOUR...BELONGINGS... WITH...YOU.'

19

'Excuse me.'

The guard at the barrier raises his chin slightly to show that he's listening, but doesn't speak.

'Can you tell me which exit I want for Balerno Crescent, please?' I ask.

He pulls the corners of his mouth down and shakes his head.

'No idea, sorry.'

Not very helpful. I stand just inside one of the exits. There are at least two – that's what's confusing me. Dru circled my dad's street, Balerno Crescent. I remember that it isn't far from the station, but I'm not sure which exit I should use to make sure I'm heading the right way.

The pouring rain makes people walk even faster and not look where they're going. The street and the station entrance are HEAVING. It's fun though, just standing, watching all the wacky outfits go by, even though I'm getting bumped and jostled and shoved all the time by people in a hurry. I didn't know you could get eight-inch platform boots or that there's a hair dye the same colour as banana yoghurt, and I would never have thought of wearing three different T-shirts at the same time over a dress. I'm getting some good ideas just standing here. Music is thumping in the distance and there's a smell of frying food in the air, like a fairground.

I get nudged a lot as I slip off my backpack, put it between my feet and bend down to pull out the map. Someone knocks me quite hard as I lean out into the rain to try and read a road sign. It's an accident – he's just rushing for a train – but I have to take a step back to stop myself falling over. And in THAT moment, while I'm looking at the map and steadying myself, another man runs in front of me, SCOOPS up my bag, FLIES across the pelican crossing and disappears down a side street. It takes a second before I realise what's happened, then I **SCREAM** and belt after him into the dark and rain.

I hear myself shouting **OVER AND OVER**, 'He's got my **BAG!** He's got my **BAG! HE'S GOT MY BAG!'**

A few people turn to look. One or two even stop walking for a moment. But no one grabs him. I spot him vanishing around a corner and race after him again, ignoring the soaking rain and deep, splashing puddles. He's difficult to see because he's so ordinary – jeans and a dark jacket, short brown hair and white trainers. By the time I've chased him around a second corner my heart is banging and I can't get my breath because of the fear sticking in my throat and the shock rattling through me. I stand, panting and squinting down the next street, trying to see him. **EVERYTHING HAS GONE! MY PHONE! MY PURSE! MY MONEY! MY BUS TICKET! DAD'S ADDRESS! MY STUFF! ALL MY STUFF!**

In less than thirty seconds the whole plan has gone BADLY, SCARILY wrong. I'm GASPING AND SWEATY AND I WANT TO THROW UP. Hundreds of people are walking past me on both sides. They have no idea that the bottom has just dropped out of my life. I'm panic breathing, IN, OUT, IN, OUT. Shallow breaths get stuck at the top of my throat, then a whimpering noise – the beginning of tears – squeaks out of me as I turn quickly around, one way, then the other, searching the crowd for anyone who looks helpful or kind. Why didn't ANYONE stop him? Didn't they HEAR what I'd been shouting? No one takes any notice of me. **NOT ONE OF THEM**. To them, I'm just a little kid out late. I'm almost invisible.

The dirty city rain runs down my back. I'm shaking with the shock of it and with the chill from my wet clothes. Why doesn't Mum or Dru or Dad, or someone, ANYONE, come and rescue me? But of course, they can't. I'm on my own.

Leaning against the nearest wall, I pull my hands inside my sweatshirt sleeves and slide down to a crouch, surrounded by a soggy sea of litter.

EVERYTHING I need was in that bag. Now I have:

- No phone, so I can't contact anyone – not Dru, not Dad, not ANYONE.
- No clothes or toothbrush, so I can't get dry or clean even if I had somewhere to go.
- No money, so I can't eat anything.

And worst of all, my map is soaked with rain. The ink has run and the paper is disintegrating in my hand. I try to smooth it out, but it's too badly damaged. I can't even find the way to Dad's house. I tug my sweatshirt hood right over my head and cup my hands over my ears to block out the rain and the people going past.

It's pitch-dark under my hood. No one will see me cry.

After a good ten minutes of snivelling and sobbing and wiping my nose on my sleeve, I slide back up the wall and stand straight again. 'Deep breath, Cordelia Codd. Get on with it,' I tell myself. You can't just melt into the pavement, you HAVE to try and find your dad.

The rain is now a fine drizzle. My jeans and top are heavy with water and my trainers squelch when I take a few steps forward and look back towards where I thought the station was. I can't see it, so I shuffle miserably to the end of the street and look around. The station isn't on the next corner, either. How many corners did I turn while I was chasing that CREEP? I just belted after him without thinking where I was going. This is Horlick Street – there's a sign across from where I'm standing. I don't remember seeing Horlick Street on the map. I'll have to start asking people.

A man and a woman about the same age as

Mum are about to pass me. They look fairly normal.

'Excuse me.'

At first they don't speak and I don't think they're going to stop. They look me up and down.

'Can you tell me where Balerno Crescent is, please?'

They look at each other, screw their noses up and shake their heads.

'Sorry, we don't live round here.'

I ask the next couple who go by. It feels safer asking couples than people on their own, or men in groups. These two are a lot younger than Mum.

'Excuse me.'

The man shouts right in my face REALLY RUDELY.

'No. I *haven't* got any money. *Clear off!*'

And they walk away with their arms around each other.

They thought I was BEGGING! I start to get really stewed up and FUMING about this, but then I look down at myself. No coat, no bag, hanging about, soaked through and I expect they thought I'm far too young to be out this late at night. NO WONDER.

I decide to ask once more and I spot an old

man tottering by with a walking stick. He looks harmless enough so I go up to him.

'Excuse me. Could you tell me…?'

'BOG OFF!' he shouts.

I step back, blinking with shock as he scuttles away, the GRIZZLY OLD TORTOISE. People here are even ruder than at school. Then a voice comes out of a doorway beside me. It's too dark to see his face at first, but it's a man's voice.

'Balerno Crescent, is it?'

I peer into the shadowy doorway, but don't go any nearer. A tall man steps out, older than the boys in the sixth form, but nowhere near as old as my dad. He's wearing quite boring clothes for round here, just a sweatshirt and jeans, and he's very thin. When he steps into the streetlight I notice that he has big dark rings around his eyes. He nods towards the other side of a pelican crossing that's nearby, pointing to a side road between a tattoo studio and a shop with black plastic clothes in the window.

'Go down there, take the first right. It's two streets after that on the left. I'll show you if you like.'

He smiles at me. He hasn't got many teeth.

'Is that where you live?' he asks, trying to be friendly, which I don't want.

I shake my head.

'My dad.'

He takes a step towards me.

'Need a lighter?'

He twitches his chin towards the doorway where there's a tray of coloured plastic cigarette lighters. I shake my head again. He gives me a weird feeling that's getting stronger by the second. He's creepy, but not in the same way that boys at school like Dean Frampton are. This man feels dangerous. Dean was just a stupid little boy.

'No. No, thanks. I have to get to my dad's.'

'D'you live with your dad, then?'

'No. I've come to find him.'

'Why? Is he lost?'

'Sort of.'

'Need a lighter?' he asks again.

'No.'

He pauses.

'Need anything else?'

He raises his eyebrows when he says this.

I don't know what he means, but I don't think it's anything good. It's probably drugs, and I'm not THAT stupid. He can probably tell I'm in a bit of trouble and a warning siren is BLARING in my head.

I frown at him.

'No. I don't need anything, thanks.'

I go to cross the road and leave him, but he picks up the tray of lighters and steps along beside me, saying again, 'I'll show you the way.'

It doesn't feel right AT ALL and I wish Dru was here. She'd know what to do.

'No. That's OK. I'm fine, thanks,' I say, and walk a bit faster.

'We can stop off at my mate's house. He's having a bit of a party.'

Then I KNOW that I just want to get away from him as fast as possible.

'No, thanks. My dad's expecting me.'

It seems a good idea to lie about that, as protection.

'We could just drop in for a while. It'll be a good party, lots of new mates. Have a drink. Have a beer. D'you like beer? Or vodka? He's always got loads of drink in. Just for a bit, eh? C'mon.'

My heart is really THUMPING now and I want to run like mad. Then he tries to hold my hand and I snatch it back.

'I don't think so,' I say.

He takes hold of my hand again and my old

RED RAGE flashes up. I kick him **HARD** in the shin, then knock his tray of lighters flying and run across the road, nearly getting hit by a taxi. The driver leans out and swears at me, but I ignore him and RUN and I can hear Dru cheering me on in my head, saying, 'RUN, Cordelia! KEEP RUNNING!' And I do. I LEG IT down the narrow street, my knees wobbling because I'm SO SCARED that he might be coming after me. I look back quickly. He's left his lighters and crossed the road. He's watching me, watching where I'm going. There are streetlights along the road, but no people now, not down here, and lots of dark doorways. I repeat his directions as I run. FIRST LEFT, SECOND RIGHT. NO, NO, FIRST RIGHT, SECOND LEFT. FIRST RIGHT, SECOND LEFT.

I look over my shoulder again.

OH NO!

He's still walking fast in my direction.

I take the first right. After the corner I sneak another look back.

He's knocking on a door. Light spills out onto the pavement for a moment as another man lets him into a house, then it's dark again as the door is quickly closed to keep the weather out.

PHEW! Looks like he isn't going to bother with me. CORDELIA CODD, YOU HAD A NARROW ESCAPE THERE!

I keep jogging. I'm desperate to get somewhere where I feel safe. After the second left turning, I stop to catch my breath, resting my back against a wall covered in graffiti. A group of older girls go by. They're laughing and chattering loudly, tottering about on high heels and holding their handbags over their heads like umbrellas.

I will NEVER drink until I fall off my shoes.

Wobbling on high heels while your tummy jiggles about is DEFINITELY a ZERO GLAMOUR SCORE. I'm quite surprised at myself for even noticing things like that when I'm in such a DIRE situation. This cheers me up a bit. Today might be DRASTIC AND DREADFUL, but I'm still the same Cordelia underneath and I WILL get out of this SOMEHOW. I know I will. It's just that RIGHT NOW, I'm not sure how or when.

The street goes quiet again when the big girls have passed. In the distance, ambulance sirens are squealing and wailing. Music is thudding out of a house nearby, but I can't make out what it is, I can only hear the CHUG^{GAH}-BAH, CHUG^{GAH}-BAH of a base line.

There are no signs for Balerno Crescent. This is Kendal Road. I move on. The rain is starting to get heavy again. The whole length of Kendal Road is quiet. It's mostly old houses with a few shops in between that have metal shutters padlocked down over their windows for the night. All the shutters are covered in spray-painted squiggles and initials and swear words that make everything look GRIM. I begin to think that the skanky-weirdo with the lighters has given me the wrong directions. What if he's just gone into that house for a moment to get his mates, and now they're out looking for me? What if they've taken another route around and are going to jump out on me? Maybe it's time to find a police station. But then Mum would get a phone call from the police that would FREAK HER THROUGH TO FRIDAY. The stress would make her even MORE poorly.

Then I see it! And my heart does a somersault. BALERNO CRESCENT. Some of the letters are broken, the 'B' is missing completely and the whole sign is nearly hidden behind a huge weed growing out of the pavement.

Now I just have to remember which number Dad lives at.

20

I know it's a hundred-and-something, but I can't remember the last two numbers. If Dru were here she'd remember it, no problem.

175? No, that's not it, no 5s in it.

143? No, no 4s in it.

187? No, no 8s in it, either.

It's no use pretending that I can remember. I walk along to the one hundred-and-somethings and stop for a moment. Maybe I can try climbing the steps to each front door and reading the names next to the doorbells.

After six or seven goes at this it's clear that not everyone puts their name or flat number next to their doorbell. It's too dark to see some of them anyway and I can't ring them all at this time of night to try and find Dad or the whole neighbourhood will be awake and FURIOUS with me for disturbing them. Besides, there could be all sorts of oddballs and mass murderers and FREAKY DEAKY DANGEROUS TYPES behind those doors – who wants to bring THEM out in the dark?

At the top of the seventh or eighth set of steps, I look up and down the road again. The rain is running in streams down my neck. I can feel it sliding the length of my back, right down to my knickers.

GREAT! I'm lost, scared AND I have wet pants.

A little further along the road there's a light on, then it's off, then it's on again. It's the only moving thing on the street, so I make my way towards it. The light turns out to be the faulty sign above a launderette. It stutters on and off, and on and off, making fizzy, sparking sounds. I read the broken yellow and red letters hanging over the big window.

On the glass door, scribbled in capitals across a piece of paper in smudgy red felt pen, a sign says:

OPEN 24 HOURS
COIN OP
NO DOGS
NO SMOKING

I can see that the place is empty, so I push the door open. It squeaks over a damp rubber mat inside. I wipe my feet, which is a bit pointless because rainwater starts draining off me, making pools on the floor. One bare light bulb hangs from the wooden ceiling. The big drums of the dryers and the huge yellow washing machines are still, like sleeping robots. Some of the washer lids have been left up. A couple of the dryer doors swing open. There's a smell of soap and newspaper ink. At the far end, out of sight of the door, there's a slatted wooden bench, like the ones in the changing rooms at school.

Along the walls above the washing machines are adverts stuck with tape.

I sit on the bench and lean my shoulder against the wall. I feel safe here. No one can see me from the street. It's warm and dry, and I soon start sliding down the bench until I'm lying on it. When the daylight comes, I think to myself, I'll be able to ask people if they know my dad's house, and I'll be able to see the door numbers and read the names next to the bells. In daylight, which is only a few hours away.

BANDI'S FRIED CHICKEN TAKE-AWAY

* FREE FRIES AND DIPS *

TEL: 0207 751 6332

Sue's Home Hairdressing

A snip at half the price
50% discount for pensioners and students

tel: 0207 901 2248

ELVIS CABS
The King of taxi services

tel: 0207 646 6572

Room to Rent
Suit non-smoking veggie
Must be dog-lover

mob: 07865 232 920

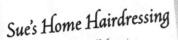

The sound of the door scraping across the rubber mat wakes me up a long time later. A man shuffles in and my heart immediately starts thumping with fear as I remember where I am and the scary mess I'm in. I don't move. Maybe he won't notice me. He's complaining to himself about the stiff hinges and the puddles on the floor and he's carrying a big black bin liner full of stuff. My eyes are open a tiny slit, so that I can close them again quickly and pretend to be asleep if he spots me.

The man lifts the lids on two of the washing machines and starts loading clothes into them from the bin liner, dropping white things into one machine and coloured things into the other. He pulls out a box of soap powder and a heavy-looking bottle of blue fabric softener. It's the same sort we use at home.

By now I've forgotten about pretending to be asleep. I'm starting to sit up silently and my eyes are properly open. I'm confused. Perhaps I'm still asleep and having a dream. The man rummages through his pockets and finds a handful of coins, which he sorts through and starts to feed into the sliding trays at the front of the two machines. I'm standing up now and stepping towards him, staring at his profile. He looks unhappy. He has no idea that anyone is here yet because he's concentrating so hard on getting his washing started. When he pushes the coins in and presses the buttons there's a whooshing and pumping sound from the first machine as it starts to suck water in through the pipes.

Now I'm less than two metres from him, but he's still concentrating on his handful of change and on selecting the right buttons for his wash. He puts money into the second machine, presses, and the same whoosh and pump begins inside it. Now that I'm certain that I'm awake and that I haven't made a mistake, I speak to him, but not how I thought I would. Not angry. Just flat words.

'I've come to get you, Dad.'

Dad spins around to look at me and immediately goes into shock. He looks terrified, like I'm a ghost. He's as white as a bed sheet and keeps saying, 'Oh-my-God-oh-my-God-oh-my-God,' and, 'Where's-your-mum-where's-your-mum-where's-your-mum?' And looking around. Not surprising, I suppose. Then, as he's having his stressy flip-out, I start to feel dizzy and shaky and I think I faint because the next thing I know I'm being carried up some stairs and I can see corners of blue, stripy wallpaper peeling off near a ceiling, drooping away from the wall like dirty flower petals.

Dad puts me down to open his front door and

then leads me straight through to the bathroom and starts running a bath while I sit on the loo with the lid down watching him. I'm not able to say much apart from, 'Did I faint?'

'Yes. You must be hungry. Are you?'

I nod.

'And you've probably caught a cold in those wet things.'

Although I feel terrible I haven't forgotten about THE EVIL JANET. I check around. There's nothing girly in the bathroom – no pink bath bubbles or make-up – and only one toothbrush. DEFINITELY a good sign. Might as well come straight out with it.

'Where's your friend?' I ask, trying to make it sound casual and not something that has made me contemplate murder.

Dad looks up quickly from where he's crouched beside the bathtub, feeling the water temperature. He hesitates, then stares back down into the water and swirls it around, holding his shirtsleeve out of the way with his dry hand.

'It… Er… It didn't work out between us.'

I don't say 'GOOD, that's one less person I have to kill', but I think it VERY LOUDLY inside my head. That's all the information I need on the subject of THE EVIL JANET.

She's GONE.

She's OFF THE SCENE.

YES! YES! YES!

All I say out loud is a quiet, 'Oh.' I nod, like I understand, and take the big green bath towel and the blue bathrobe that Dad hands me from his airing cupboard. He looks like he hasn't slept for ages. He's got more wrinkles than before and he needs a haircut.

'There's shampoo and soap and stuff on the shelf above you,' he says. Then he sighs. 'Oh, Coco. What were you thinking, coming all this way alone?'

I tell him about having to come and get him because we need him at home and about having my bag nicked, but I think my words get mixed up because I'm SO tired now.

'It would all have been fine if my bag hadn't been stolen,' I say.

He runs his hand over my head, smiles a sort of sad smile and says, 'Thank you, Coco.'

I'm not sure what he's thanking me for. I don't quite understand. Grown-ups can be so MUDDLING sometimes.

'Have a bit of a soak and I'll take your stuff down to the dryer. The bakery will be open. I'll bring us some breakfast treats, shall I? Then we'll talk some more, or you can sleep first.'

I nod and shoo him out of the bathroom saying, 'I'm too big to have company in here, now.'

He shuffles out awkwardly, but very quickly. 'Sorry, yes. Just pass your things out.'

Dad's shampoo makes quite good bath foam. I bubble all over and get a good lather going on the surface of the steamy water, then sink down and relax. My muscles ache as if I'm as old as Granny Twigg. This feels SO lovely that I cry a little bit with relief. It was a scary night and NO mistake. But then I think of Dru and I hope she's not too FRANTIC PANTS with worry, and I'm calling her in my head shouting, 'I FOUND him, Dru! I FOUND him! First part of the mission ACCOMPLISHED.'

When I hear Dad opening the front door I wake up from a doze.

'I'm back. You still in there?' he calls.

'Just getting out,' I call back as I slowly climb

onto the bath mat and wrap myself in the huge towel. I'm too tired to rub myself dry so I just dab all over, but I stop to listen when I hear voices.

Dad is on the phone.

He isn't whispering, but the phone is at the other end of the flat, so it's hard to make out what's being said, even when I open the bathroom door quite wide. I catch the words 'last night' and 'she' and 'fine, don't worry'. There are long pauses where Dad is silent, like he's listening to the person on the other end. I know it must be Mum he's talking to. Then he pushes the living-room door closed very gently and his voice goes quieter, so I don't hear any more. I shut myself in the bathroom again and attack the tangles in my hair with Dad's HORRID plastic comb, which is all I can find. When I'm dry, I put on the big blue bathrobe and knock on the living-room door. I hear Dad sniff. He opens the door and I notice that his eyes are pink round the edges as if he's been crying, but he claps his hands together when I walk in and smiles.

'All clean?'

'Very.'

'Let's have breakfast then,' he says.

My tummy is so empty that we can both hear it

rumbling. I sit down in Dad's tiny kitchen at a little round table with a glass top. It wobbles when I lean on it. The kitchen clock says eight-fifteen. I MUST call Dru.

Dad tugs open the door of his ancient oven. WONDERFUL smells drift towards me. He does his funny waiter act.

'Today, mademoiselle, we 'ave fresh, warm bagels with smoked salmon and cream cheese. Or, if you prefer, we 'ave croissant with jam or pain au chocolat.'

'I'll have everything on the menu, please,' I say, shaking out the piece of kitchen roll he has laid out as a napkin, 'starting with bagels.'

Dad tucks into a plateful of croissants and pours tea for me (Earl Grey), and strong black coffee for himself. After a few minutes he sits back and says, 'I spoke to Mum just now.'

I try not to sound like I already know.

'Oh. Is she cross?'

'She was **very concerned** about what you've done, coming here.'

I chew more slowly. This is a way to show grown-ups that you're listening.

'She told me about having to leave work.' He

215

pauses. 'I didn't know about that… Or about her being…needing a rest.'

I keep chewing and nod a lot, hoping that he'll carry on telling me more about what he and Mum have discussed.

'I managed to reassure her that you're fine and that you'll be home by tonight.'

'So, are you're coming home to look after her?' I ask, pushing it.

He sighs and shakes his head.

'That's not what I said.'

I put my bagel down and fold my arms. He leans forward and balances his elbows on the table, sliding his plate out of the way first.

'I'm *truly* sorry that I can't be there with you, Coco. I couldn't be more sorry about anything, *anything*. Believe me. Please try to forgive me for being such a crap dad.'

I can see that he means it, but 'sorry' WON'T DO. 'Sorry' is not the answer I want. My life is a PILE OF PLOP because of the things my parents can't do or won't do. I feel my RED RAGE bubbling up and I start shouting about losing all my friends because I was so grumpy and miserable, and about Ellie Simmons with her bogey, and about

Miss Haliborn being OUTRAGEOUSLY unfair, and about all the detentions and my terrible school report. I yell at him about all the things I have to do in the house now, and all the things I CAN'T do and Mum CAN'T do so they just get left, and how I was too embarrassed to have Dru around because of the mess but she saw it anyway because Mum was stuck under the table and that saying he's sorry is NOT GOOD ENOUGH!

'And THAT'S what it's been like for ME while you've been away.'

I've gone completely off my bagel. Dad has left the best bit of his croissant, the pointy corner that's always the most crusty and buttery part.

'Coco, I'm not a bad man,' he says. 'But I *am* a *very stupid* one sometimes, like all adults. It's just that I've been *more* stupid than most. I had *no idea* that things had been so difficult. How could I when Mum didn't tell me?'

'Why didn't she tell you?'

'I expect she was too proud. She probably wanted to prove that she could manage fine without me.'

He pushes croissant crumbs around the plate with his finger.

'Well, now you know. And your girlfriend's

217

DUMPED you, so why can't you come home and look after Mum and me?'

He breathes in quickly, like I just poked him hard in the ribs and it hurt and he's going 'ouch!'. I know it was a mean thing to say, but I wanted it to hurt. He doesn't get cross with me, though. He just points out a few things.

'Mum might not want me there. I might be the last person in the world she wants to take care of her.'

'You KNOW Mum wants you to come home. You're just a BIG CHICKEN because you'll have to say sorry to her and be nice to her and you're too scared to do that.'

He just nods and goes to start the washing-up. If he's cross with me, he really shouldn't be. In fact, how DARE he? He can't be cross with me EVER AGAIN after what he's done. I'M the furious one.

I go off in a bit of a huff and lie curled up on the sofa for ages. Despite being SO furious with Dad, I can't help relaxing as I listen to the sound of him washing up. If I keep my eyes shut, I can pretend we're back at home and he's clearing up in our kitchen with Mum.

21

By the time I wake up it's nearly afternoon and I
STILL haven't rung Dru. Dad says I can use his
mobile to call Dru AFTER I call Mum. Mum is a
bit tearful on the phone, but she doesn't have a full-
blown SOB-A-THON, like I'd expected.

'You gave me a fright, y'know,' she says.

'I didn't mean to. If everything had gone
according to plan I'd have been back before you
knew I'd gone.'

'That's not the point,' Mum says. 'I have to be
able to trust you, Coco, and it's going to be a while
before I can do that again.'

I can just see her, rolling her eyes to the ceiling
and shaking her head.

'I'm sorry,' I say, and I mean it, 'but…'

'No buts. Don't *ever* pull a trick like this again. *Anything* could have happened to you. And I've spoken to Drusilla's mum. Honestly, I'm *so* surprised at a sensible girl like her.'

'Is she in trouble?'

'You bet she is, young lady. She'll probably be grounded for a long time.'

Poor Dru. It's all my fault – me and my weird family. I back down and apologise again. But I KNOW that this is my ONLY chance of getting Dad back so I'm not as sorry as I sound. Sometimes you have to let adults think they know what's best and that you're GENUINELY LISTENING to their advice so that they don't get into a STRESS-O-MATIC CONTROL FIT. This is one of those moments. I change the subject from me and Dru to Mum and Dad as soon as I think I can get away with it.

'Mum… Will you ask Dad to come back?'

There's a pause. I hear her sigh.

'I don't think so, Coco. Your dad and I have a lot to talk about.'

'Does that mean there's a possibility, when you've had a talk?'

'That means what it means, Coco. It means, "I don't think so".'

But I think she means 'maybe'. Otherwise, wouldn't she say *Absolutely not, no way,* NEVER', or something more definite sounding?

'Please don't get your hopes up, love. I know you think it would all be fine if Dad were back with us, but it's a lot more complicated than you realise.'

I want to say, 'I know all about complicated, THANK YOU VERY MUCH. Try having MY life to deal with.' But she sounds really tired now and I'm pretty sleepy again myself. Carrying upsetting stuff around is EXHAUSTING, like having your pockets full of potatoes ALL THE TIME.

I get Drusilla's landline number from Mum because I can't remember it off by heart and ring her as soon as Mum has said 'love you, Coco' and I've said 'love you, too' and we've hung up very gently because we know that we need to be SUPER CAREFUL with each other's feelings, even without saying so.

Dru answers the phone straight away, breathless, like she knew it was me and has just bombed down the stairs.

'Hi.'

221

'Dru? I'm OK. I couldn't call, I'm SO sorry. I'm at Dad's. You won't believe…I had ALL my stuff nicked….'

I tell her EVERYTHING. A good ten minutes goes by with me jabbering on before I pause to catch my breath.

'Are you there, Dru?'

'Yeah, I'm here. I'm listening. Wow! I was *manic panic girl* when there was no text this morning. Phew! I mean, wow! I'm just so glad you haven't been murdered or anything cos I'd feel like I'd sent you to your *death*. Sounds like there's been progress with those parents of yours, though.'

'D'you think so, really? You don't think I'm being too optimistic?'

'There's no such thing as too optimistic. That's what my aunt Zillah says. Hang in there, and get your dad back here fast, even if you have to knock him out and post him home. Did you tell him about that guy your mum had a date with?'

'The sea mammal? The Walrus? No. Should I?'

'A little bit of jealousy might help.'

'What if he doesn't get jealous?'

'Then we'll think of something else. Try it!'

Dad has just finished in the shower so I tell Dru I

have to go because I want to get to work on this idea straight away. I've forgotten about being tired now.

This HAS to work. I am NOT going to spend the rest of my life with Dad living two hundred miles away and Mum crying under the table while the house falls apart. I will NOT have that life. What sort of start in the world would that give to the **GREATEST** **costume designer in the history of cinema?**

One of Dad's amazing salads is waiting on the table for lunch. The smells of basil and tomatoes and lemon dressing drift around the kitchen. There's crusty French bread and butter, three different cheeses, olives and dates and almonds. It's a typical 'Dad lunch', just like they used to be at home. I break off a piece of bread and dip it into a puddle of olive oil on my plate. 'I've missed your food SO much, Dad.'

He smiles, but he's a bit quiet. I suppose I have been a bit narky with him. He's probably wondering what's going to come out of my mouth next. He looks tired and stubbly round the chin.

'When did you last have a shave?' I ask. 'Your chin looks like a badger's bum.'

Dad gives a little laugh.

'Oh, nice language,' he says. 'Is that what they teach you at school?'

'That's nothing!'

If ONLY he knew. The language you hear on a normal day at Beckmere would turn milk into lumpy cheese.

'Have we got time to get you a haircut, too?' I ask.

Dad runs his hand over his head. SHOCKINGLY bad style, I think to myself. When men start going bald they should just shave it off.

'It looked better before,' I say, 'when it was like a tennis ball. You don't want to end up looking like Terry Snaul.'

Dad laughs at the name.

'Who's that?'

'Oh, just some bloke from work who took Mum out for dinner,' I say, ever so casually.

Dad leans back.

'Oh, yes?'

I don't look at him as I scoop up another piece of smelly Camembert cheese and squash it onto a chunk of bread. Dad's curious, I can tell, so I say a bit more.

'He was HORRID. And Mum said afterwards

that he "didn't behave very nicely".

Dad's hands are on the table. One is wrapped around his glass of fruit juice, relaxed and calm. But I'm looking at the other one, which is screwed up tight so that his knuckles are white.

THAT is jealousy! That is DEFINITELY jealousy, I think to myself.

Drusilla was right again.

Dad takes a sip of juice, trying to be cool about this information, but when he swallows it makes a hard sound, like his throat is dry.

'So, she's not seeing him any more, then?' he asks.

'Oh, no. But after that he started bullying her at work. Drusilla's sister, Jess, says it was, what's the word? HARASSMENT. That's it! He was a rotten loser.'

Dad sits up straight and takes some more bread and cheese, frowning so that there are deep lines across his forehead.

'Really? I didn't know about that… I thought she was just very tired…'

Suddenly, I can't stop my temper. It flashes out again, like a snake tongue.

'Of course you don't KNOW, you're not THERE, are you? And if you HAD been there she wouldn't have gone out with the GREAT GREASY WALRUS in the first place.'

He raises his hands gently.

'OK, don't get angry again. These are *all* things Mum and I have to talk about. I told you, there's some stuff she hasn't told me. You've made it quite clear what you think of me and I've made it clear how bad I feel about all this. Now let's just wait until I get you home and I can chat with Mum, OK?'

I pull my mouth about in a twisty, 'Oh, all right then' sort of way.

He raises his eyebrows.

'And I expect I can pop in somewhere and get a haircut so you're not too ashamed of me. I just haven't got around to–'

'To looking after yourself?' I look around the pokey kitchen. 'I can see that.'

Dad smiles to himself as he butters a bit more bread.

'You wait until you're a student. You might have to live somewhere much worse than this.' He points towards a big patch of damp on the wall with his knife. 'I'll come round and screw my nose up at your peeling wallpaper.'

Of course, I will NEVER live somewhere like

this, not even when I'm a student, but I don't want to argue with him again.

Then Dad manages to make everything OK with a BRILLIANT suggestion, one that takes my mind off the HEAVY POTATOES OF GLUMNESS in my pockets for a while.

'We've plenty of time before the bus. I thought you might like to visit a museum this afternoon. There's one not far from the station that has a big costume collection.'

My eyes open wide and my hands flap in front of me with excitement. I don't need to say anything. Dad laughs.

'I'll take that as a "yes", then? We'll go in half an hour.'

22

The Underground doesn't feel scary at all when I'm
with Dad. With him beside me I'm not frightened
of anything. We have to change to a different line
at Leicester Square. It's HEAVING with tourists,
so I stick to Dad like glue in case I get pushed and
jostled away in the wrong direction, but even that
doesn't bother me. It takes about half an hour to get
to our station. I count ten stops between Camden
Town and South Kensington. It's interesting
listening to all the different languages being spoken
and watching the hundreds and hundreds of faces
getting on and off the trains. I wonder about where
they're all going and whether their lives are happy
or sad.

After we get off the Underground we have to walk and walk down the LONGEST tunnel, like an enormous pipe with tiles on the inside. A busker is playing the guitar and singing a song that Dad hums along to, smiling a bit, like it reminds him of something happy. The music carries all along the tunnel and wraps itself around us so we hear it long before we pass the man playing. Dad drops a pound into his guitar case. Then we turn up some steps, cross a mad-busy road, go through a MASSIVE doorway CRAMMED with visitors, and we're suddenly there, at the Victoria and Albert Museum.

Looking up at the domed ceiling in the entrance is like standing on the inside of the MOST BEAUTIFUL Christmas bauble ever. For a few minutes I'm fine on my own, waiting for Dad to come back from the loo. White marble halls open out to both sides of me. Couples stroll through them and groups of visitors are having guided tours, chattering away in Japanese and French and German while they admire the gleaming statues that fill every space. It's magical, but I'm impatient to get going and see the costumes.

Ages pass.

I start to worry.

Dad is taking so FLIPPING long, and I know that he never gets an upset tummy because Mum used to say that Dad had insides that could process tin cans and cardboard boxes. Perhaps he's admiring the new haircut he got before we left Camden. Well, he shouldn't. Not now, not while I'm waiting for him on my own.

My forehead starts to feel warm and sweaty and my insides are turning over like I might be sick. Then my breathing gets quicker. I'm panicking. Has he left me again? I twizzle around to search for him, straining my eyes in every direction, starting to shake and cry. Has anyone noticed my sweatiness and weird breathing? Do they show on the outside? I start to look for a corner to curl up in. Then suddenly, he's here! When he sees my scared face, his smile drops and he has a seriously worried look.

'Coco, I'm *so* sorry. There was a terrible queue.'

I don't believe him.

How could he leave me alone for so long when I've only just found him? How could he do that when he needs to be extra careful with my feelings today? I scream at him because I was SO frightened that he'd left me again.

'There's NEVER a queue in MEN'S TOILETS.

EVERYONE knows that.'

My shout echoes around the museum. Dozens
of people stop dead and turn to look at the screaming
brat. Dad blushes and presses his finger to his lips to
try and shush me. He puts his hands on my shoulders
and I almost shrug them off and flounce away, but
he whispers, 'I popped into the gift shop as well.
The queue was in the shop, not the loo. I wanted to
make sure you had this before we went in to see the
costumes.'

He hands me a heavy paper bag. I take it,
cautiously, and peep inside. Dad has bought me the
MOST glamorous sketchbook in the universe.

I feel ASHAMED of my tantrum and mumble,
'Sorry. Thank you. Sorry. It's lovely! I was scared. Sorry.'

He gives me a long hug and a kiss on my forehead.
'It's OK. Coco,' he says. 'I understand.'

And I think he does understand a bit. I think he
knows now what a FUDGE UP he's made of my
head, and for the rest of the visit he stays very close
to me.

The cover of the sketchbook is black and smooth,
like panther skin. A fat red ribbon ties it shut. Beside
it in the bag is a set of pencils, six of them, from hard
grey for tiny lines, to super soft and velvety black for

smudging. They all fit into a pencil case that matches the sketchbook, soft and black with a red zip and a diamante pattern down the side.

'I thought you might want to draw some of the costumes,' Dad says.

I stroke the GORGEOUS pencil case and the sleek sketchbook and kiss him on the cheek, and then we step into the DIVINE WARDROBE of the costume collection.

For two hours, I am served up a giant helping of GLAMOUR. It's as if all the most beautiful clothes in the world have been brought out just for me, to take my mind off what could have been another super weird and scary day.

Dad stays close behind me while I gaze into the glass cases. Some of the dresses are two hundred years old and SO delicate and complicated that they look like they were made by pixies.

I make a long, long list of all the new words, words as tasty as the most delicious food. I don't want to forget ANYTHING.

- silk organdie
- silk satin
- silk damask
- silk velvet

- silk chiffon
- black taffeta
- blonde lace
- tweed lined with sateen
- silk jersey
- beaded tulle
- marabou feathers

And the names of designers! Dad helps me to pronounce them properly. I will say them out loud to myself on rainy days, to cheer myself up.

Pierre Cardin (pee-air car-dan)
Hardy Amies (har-dee ay-mis)
Fortuny (for-too-nee)
Christian Lacroix (cris-tee-ann la-crwah)
Yves Saint Laurent (eve san-law-ron)
Balenciaga (bal-en-thee-ah-ga)

And my favourite,

Hubert de Givenchy (ooh-bear duh ji-von-shee).

Even the underwear has interesting names.

<u>Waspie</u> – this pulls your middle in to make it look tiny

<u>Cage crinoline</u> – a bit like wearing a giant birdcage to make your petticoat stick out

<u>Bustle</u> – a sort of cushion that ladies wore under a long skirt to make their bums stick out. Sticky-out bums were very fashionable once.

<u>Chemise</u> – a little top to go under a blouse.

All I see in the shops on the high street are dull, frumpy names for things like skirt, jumper and jeans. Most of the clothes on display here people just don't wear any more. I scribble the names of these down, too, and tell myself I will learn them by heart to be ready for when I'm designing costumes for historical films.

<u>Banyan</u> – a long, fancy dressing gown.
<u>Dolman</u> – a short jacket that went over a dress with a bustle.

Frock coat – a long coat for men.
Tail coat – a coat that is long, but only at the back, for men.
Mantua – a **very** fancy dress for meeting the king or queen.

Riding habit – a long skirt and jacket for riding side-saddle in.

(Looks **uncomfortable!**)
Tea gown – a pretty dress for afternoons.

And there are more French words that I have to get Dad to read out. He knows a lot of French and Italian words.

Haute couture (oat-coot-your)
Couturier (coot-your-ee-ay)
Chenille (shen-eel)
Voile (vwal)

I make a few quick drawings and take longer over one particular dress. It is the most elegant dress EVER IN THE HISTORY OF DRESSES. It has no frills or flouncy bits and it is as black and sleek as my new pencil case. All around the neck are rows and rows of pearls in a semi-circle, like an Egyptian queen would wear. I sigh all the time as I draw it with my blackest pencil.

Dad gives me lots of attention, never leaving me for a moment. I forget that up ahead there are those SERIOUS CONVERSATIONS that Mum and Dad need to have. Eventually, he touches my shoulder and says, 'Time to go, sweetheart.'

It's SO difficult to tear myself away, SO hard to zip those pencils into their lovely case and slip the sketchbook back into the thick paper bag.

But what is coming next is even more amazing. My parents will be meeting each other for the first time in MONTHS.

23

We have the last empty seats on the bus. Dad sits by the aisle so that he can stretch his legs and I sit by the window so that I can watch the view.

Dad has packed one of his 'travelling snacks', which means a FANTASTIC picnic and loads of cold juice. I'm already hungry, but Dad says we have to wait until we're on the motorway before we can eat.

Just when I think we'll never get going and I'll never get anything to eat again, the engine starts. It's a long, slow, hot journey across the city to the motorway. I even get fed up looking at all the different buildings.

Once we're on the motorway the bus speeds up and a breeze comes through the air vents. A sigh of relief goes round the bus. Babies stop fidgeting so much and adults nod off, or settle down with newspapers and books. Dad works on a sudoku puzzle for about the first half an hour of the motorway, until my stomach can't stand it any longer and I nag him about food until he gives in.

There's chicken and tomato salad with lemon and black pepper. Pudding is Belgian chocolate mousse in little cartons, and we have mango lassi to drink. While we're eating, struggling with the plastic forks he's packed, and rescuing tomato pips from our chins, Dad asks, 'How long until the school holidays now?'

I finish my mouthful of chicken and shrug, because I'm not exactly sure.

'About four weeks, I think. Not long.'

'Well, maybe we could go away somewhere together for a week or so.'

'With Mum?'

He puts his fork down in his plastic picnic box.

'It might take Mum a while before she's ready to think about having a holiday with me. It'd probably be just you and me.'

'And I'd spend all the time thinking how much better it would be if Mum was there.' I shake my head. 'No thanks.'

I go back to my salad, looking out of the window to make the point that I am NOT IMPRESSED with the suggestion of half-parent holidays. Maybe it wouldn't be so bad. It might even be fun. But it isn't what I want AT ALL. After a few minutes – in which I finish my salad and open my chocolate mousse – I ask Dad **STRAIGHT OUT AND QUICKLY** so there's no time for him to think up a 'typical parent' answer, 'Why **DID** you leave, **REALLY?**'

Dad opens his mousse and takes a spoonful. He doesn't say anything at first. He swallows that first spoonful and stares into the tub for a moment, and I'm just about to ask him again, in case he hasn't heard or is trying to ignore the question, when he says, 'Well, things got very difficult when I had to sell the restaurant.'

'What d'you mean "difficult"?'

Dad looks up at the luggage rack and crinkles his eyes, as if he has a pain somewhere or is thinking very hard. Then he looks back at his mousse.

'Well… When I lost the restaurant, I began to think I wasn't a very good chef.'

'That's STUPID. You're the best chef in the WORLD.

'But people want fast, cheap, rubbishy food and that isn't what I'm good at cooking.'

I screw my face up. Those people are STUPID, I think to myself. They deserve to be GROTESQUELY FAT and covered in spots.

'Just because they want cheap, rubbish food,' I say, 'doesn't mean cheap, rubbish food is good. That's as ridiculous as saying that BIG BAGGY BLOOMERS are cheap so I'm going to wear them.'

Dad laughs.

'You're absolutely right, Coco. But a lot of people would rather have a plateful of cheap chips than a helping of minted baby new potatoes.'

'Well, I wouldn't.'

'I know you wouldn't, sweetheart, because you're a young lady of *considerable taste and style.*'

'Like my mum,' I say, so that he'll think about Mum again.

He pauses, knowing exactly why I've said it.

'Yes, like your mum. Now eat your chocolate mousse.'

I do. But I haven't had a full answer yet.

'So, why DID you leave? You still haven't said.'

Dad sips his mango lassi, and then stares into the bottle, running his finger around the rim.

'Well. When I felt that I wasn't a very good chef, I began to think I wasn't much good at *anything*.'

'Like what?'

'Like being a husband, or a dad.'

I have just scooped the last spoonful of mousse into my mouth. It nearly gets stuck when I swallow.

'That's **STUPID**, too. Why didn't you ask **ME** if you were doing OK as a dad? I thought you were the best dad in the world until you disappeared. That's when you became **CRAP DAD OF THE CENTURY**.'

My voice has got a bit loud and an old lady sitting in front of us peers between the seats, looking at me over her glasses. She has a tight, strict face covered in pink, old-lady powder. That's what Miss Haliborn will look like when she's old, I think. The lady doesn't need to tell me off.

'Sorry,' I say.

'Sorry,' says Dad, too.

She goes back to her book.

I whisper to Dad, 'Are you having what Drusilla calls a "mid-life crisis"?'

Dad smiles and whispers back, 'Let's just call it a *bad patch*, shall we?'

BAD PATCH? More like ROTTEN CABBAGE PATCH, I think.

'Does that mean it'll get better?' I ask.

'Couldn't get much worse, could it, Coco, love?'

'I suppose not,' I say, and snuggle up to him because I don't want to be snappy with him any more, even though it's going to be difficult if he keeps talking like an IDIOT.

We've stopped. The weather has cooled down and we're at a motorway service station. Dad says I can use his mobile to check in with Dru. She answers straight away and almost shouts with excitement when I say, 'Hi, Dru. It's me.'

'Hi! Any news? Is he jealous?'

'DEFINITELY. That was a brilliant idea. It might not be enough to make him decide to stay, though. Any more suggestions before we get back on the bus?'

Drusilla takes a deep breath and makes a thinking noise – a sort of humming, like a fridge. After a few seconds she says, 'So, he hasn't said anything about staying yet?'

'No. It's still just "no promises" and "Mum and I have to talk".'

Dru makes the humming-fridge noise again and I SWEAR I can feel the vibration of her thought machinery coming down the phone line.

'You're just going to have to tell him about Dean and those pictures.'

'I CAN'T tell my DAD about the naked picture thing! Think again, Dru. Think HARD.'

'If he'd been there when it happened, you would've told him, wouldn't you?'

'Yes, but…'

'This could clinch it. This could be what makes him decide to stay around. Imagine how bad he'll feel that he wasn't there to stick up for you.'

I bite my lip.

'But it's SO EMBARRASSING.'

'I don't think this is a time for worrying about that, Cordelia. Tell him about Dean and the pictures. What've you got to lose?'

I'm blushing at the thought. It's just too SQUIRMIFYING for words.

'Ohhhh…' I groan. 'OK…I'll try. It was just so CRINGE-MAKING that I hate even THINKING about it, never mind telling my dad.'

Dad is waving to me. He's bought me a drink.

'I've got to go. Wish me luck.'

Dad has a cup of coffee and I have an apple juice.

'We've still got five minutes,' he says. 'Shall we sit out here?'

There are benches nearby. I love that about summer, sitting outside as the sun goes down because it's warm enough and not being able to believe that winter will ever come round or that you'll EVER have to wear a big coat or gloves again.

I start by asking Dad another question because what he told me on the bus still didn't quite make sense.

'When you felt like you were useless at everything, why did you go and get a girlfriend and leave?'

Dad stops spooning the froth off his cappuccino and shakes his head.

'That's a very good question.'

He looks up at the pink clouds and sighs.

'Why? Why? Why? I think it's because, when you don't feel very good about yourself you sometimes don't behave well.'

I nod. I understand. Wasn't that exactly what I'd been doing at school? If I'd been happy would I have been horrid to Jen or shoved a bag over Ellie's head?

'Do you think unhappiness makes you see things

a bit lopsided?' I ask.

It's Dad's turn to nod.

'I think that's exactly it, Coco. But sometimes the things you do when you're unhappy hurt other people and that can take a long time to put right.'

I think about Jen and Ellie again and realise that Dru must have been able to survive all the horrid things that were said to her at school because, basically, underneath it all, she's HAPPY.

'Do you think when boys behave badly towards girls it's because they're unhappy?'

Dad frowns and asks, 'In what way?'

'OK, here goes...'

I give a little cough and begin THE STORY OF DEAN. I tell Dad how Dean invited me to Battle of the Bands and then made **DESPICABLE** pictures of me that weren't me at all just because I wouldn't snog him, and how I split his lip with a stolen boxing glove, and that he was suspended for three weeks afterwards – except I give him more details than that and once I get talking I'm not as embarrassed as I thought I'd be and I go *ON*

AND ON

AND ON like this, showing how upset and angry I still am about the whole thing.

When I finish the story Dad's mouth is hanging open slightly and his eyes are sort of glazed over because he is obviously GOB-SMACKED AND HORRIFIED, which I think is a pretty good result.

Another **genius notion** from Dru!

I spot the bus driver getting back aboard our coach and shake Dad's arm to snap him out of his shock.

'We have to go, Dad. Bring your coffee.'

We are quiet for the rest of the journey. Dad doesn't mention THE STORY OF DEAN, but I can tell that he's letting what I've told him sink in, just from something extra in his quietness. He sits very still, except for stroking my hair when I have my head on his shoulder and he thinks I'm sleeping. I doze off for some of the time, but mostly I am breathing in the smell of his clothes and the warmth coming from him. I want to stay as close to him as I can, in case the UNTHINKABLE happens and he goes away again.

24

There's a light on in the kitchen when we get back.
Mum comes to the door before we have time to
ring the bell. It's quite late and nearly dark. She isn't
in her dressing gown, though. She has one of her
pretty dresses on, and lipstick.

This is a VERY GOOD SIGN.

Mum and Dad hardly speak at first. They seem a bit uncomfortable with each other, making sure they don't stand too close together or look in each other's faces for more than a millisecond.

I hug Mum and say I'm sorry for giving her a fright, and that I'll have to go straight to bed because I'm very tired and not at all hungry. Dad is hovering in the hall with his bag. I kiss him goodnight and go upstairs. Dad follows Mum into the kitchen and closes the door. I get into my nightie, then sit at the top of the stairs hoping to hear what they're saying but it's nearly impossible because their conversation is low and whispery at first.

One or two things Mum says reach me because she starts to raise her voice. It gets gradually louder. I hear her use words that I've only heard in the playground before. Then she starts shouting. Dad's voice stays calm. He seems to be letting Mum have an explosion, AND SO HE SHOULD. I hear her yell '*IRRESPONSIBLE*' and '*DAMAGING*' and 'you have **NO** idea'. My thumping heart feels like it's making even more noise than her voice. Perhaps she's going to tell him to leave? Maybe the plan isn't going to work and we'll be back where we started. Then their voices go quiet again.

I lean my head against the banister and listen, but I can't make out the words any more. At first I'm waiting for the shouting to start again, but it doesn't. Their talking stays low and calm for a long time and just hearing them in the kitchen together is good. It's been such a long time since I heard Mum speak to anyone else late at night.

I must've fallen asleep there because I sit up with a jump when Dad comes out of the kitchen and picks up his bag.

'Where are you going?' I call out, which makes him jump because he thought I was in bed.

He whispers, 'Only to my friend Andy's house. He says I can stay over. I'll be back in the morning.'

I stand up, ready to shout at him, but I manage not to.

'Like last time?'

He frowns, but then realises that I mean 'like when you went to the conference and didn't come back'.

'No, Coco. I promise. Not like last time. I'm going to come and help your mum around the house tomorrow and we'll both be here when you get back from school, too.'

'Double promise?'

He smiles.

'Triple and quadruple promise. And I'll cook some dinner for us all. OK?'

I run down and grab another hug, just in case.

I didn't sleep very much, and I'm SO full of yawns in English this morning that Mr Grimpson keeps looking over his glasses at me and saying things like 'Perhaps the drowsy amongst us, like *Miss Cordelia Codd,* could do their best to join in with the class,' and, 'It seems to be a little too early in the morning for some of us. I refer to you, Miss Codd.' Every time he says my name I wake up with a jump and everyone laughs at me, including Dru, but I suppose it is pretty funny really.

The day goes on and on. Will the final bell EVER ring? I'm DESPERATE to get home to see what progress Mum and Dad have made.

At last it happens, school finishes, but Dru and I can't get on the first bus because it's packed like an animal truck again. AAGH! ANNOYING! So it's late when I finally run through the door to find Mum and Dad in the kitchen and FANTASTIC cooking smells in the air: apples and roast meat and some kind of sweet pudding. Mum and Dad seem quite relaxed.

RELIEF! Dad kept his promise.

Mum sends me straight round to Dru's house with a bunch of flowers for Jess saying, 'You go and apologise for running off when she was supposed to be looking after you. The poor girl was round here today, beside herself with worry because she thought she hadn't been careful enough. She'd never have forgiven herself if something had happened to you. Off you go.'

So I go, even though I don't want to leave our house when it feels so cosy again with both of them there and dinner nearly ready.

Will Dru's family be angry with me? Dru says not. They've only grounded her for a week, not for ETERNITY, like she expected. Still, I'm not sure what they'll say when they see me again.

But I can't believe how sweet they are towards me. Jess isn't angry that I ran away, just pleased that I'm back safely. She hugs me, like she was my own big sister, and nearly cries when I give her the flowers. She arranges them in a vase while Dru and I watch and both think how beautiful she is. Dru's parents come home just then. They're noisy and friendly. Her mum hugs me, too, and her dad says, 'Goodness, here's the *adventurous* one I've been hearing about,' and wags his finger at me, but he smiles too, and says I must come and stay again *very soon* as long as I promise not to run off.

Which I DO promise.

Then I say, 'See you tomorrow,' to Dru, because she and I both know that I have to get back to Mum and Dad to keep the plan on track.

'Keep me updated,' she says and gives me a little hug.

After dinner, which is a FEAST, I start questioning Mum and Dad.

'So, what's happening with you two?' I ask.

They look at each other and roll their eyes as if to say 'Who taught her to be so *direct*?'. Mum smoothes her skirt along her crossed leg and stares at the material, like she doesn't want to see my face when she says what she's going to say. Her hand is shaking a bit and that makes my he♥rt start bumping with fear so much that I think I might sick up my dinner at any moment.

'Well, tomorrow Dad has to go back to London,' she says.

NO WONDER SHE DIDN'T LOOK
STRAIGHT AT ME.

I throw my dessert spoon across the kitchen
and we all freeze for a second, listening to it bounce
with a metal

cling   clang   b...b...b...boing!

off the wall and onto the floor tiles. Mr Belly
screeches and runs under the table.

Then I scream at them.

'*NO!*'

Dad starts making 'calm down' gestures with
his hands.

'*NO!!*' I yell even louder, so that Mum winces. 'I
did **NOT** go all that way to get him so that he could
disappear again.'

Mum is holding the tops of her arms now, as if
she's cold, but she can't be because it's summer and
the kitchen is warm. She's trying to look at me and
not cry. Dad carries on where she left off.

'Hold on a minute. Let us tell you the whole
story.'

I tuck my hands into my armpits and scowl
HARD, but I get gradually less sCRUNCHED UP

and FOUL-FACED as he explains.

'I have to go back and hand my notice in at work. Then I'm going to come back up here and look for a job so that I can be closer to you and Mum. Andy says I can stay in his spare room for a while.'

I am even more cautious than Mr Belly, who is poking his nose out from under the table to see if it's 'all clear'.

'I don't believe you'll come back,' I say.

'You'll *have* to *trust* me and be *patient*, Coco. I'll be back in a couple of weeks at the most and I'll call you every day until then, if you want.'

'You'd BETTER. And I WON'T trust you until you DO come back and tell me you've got a job and you're STAYING.'

'I understand that, Coco, and I won't let you down.'

'We'll see,' I say.

I don't understand how Mum can be SO SURE that Dad means what he says but when I ask her later on, as I'm going up to bed, she just strokes my head and whispers, 'Give him a chance, Coco. Be patient.'

And he does ring, EVERY night, like he promised.

Mum is still tired, but she smiles more and is always up and dressed in the mornings with a bit of make-up on. I don't have to worry about the laundry or ironing much because she does most of that, too, but I still help because I don't think it's fair to let Mum slip back into doing everything for me just because she's feeling stronger.

Sometimes I worry about the change in her. I mean, how can I tell if she's REALLY getting better and not just pretending so that I won't be upset? But when I tell Dru this she reminds me to stay OPTIMISTIC. So I try to think only good thoughts about where this will all end up.

25

It's been nearly two weeks since we said goodbye to Dad. He should be back any day now. But right in the middle of all my stressing about whether he'll keep his promise, Dru goes and drops another bucket load of worry on me.

We're sitting on the playing field after lunch, tugging at blades of grass and talking about a television programme we both saw, agreeing that it was TOTAL dog poo and wondering why we COMPLETELY WASTED thirty minutes of our lives watching it. Dru suddenly goes quiet, then just comes out with, 'I have some news. I think it's bad.'

I sit up and spit out the blade of grass I've been sliding between the gaps in my teeth.

'What?'

'My family are moving back to the States. It's because of Dad's work. We're going in a couple of weeks.'

'*WHAT!? HOW CAN THEY DO THAT?*'

Dru nods.

'I know. It *stinks*. And I'm *so* sorry. I feel *really* bad, like I'm deserting you in your *hour of need* or something, and you're the first friend I've made here. It *stinks*,' she says again, throwing a bunch of grass that goes nowhere, just flies around in the breeze. 'I gave Mom and Dad a big row about it, but they won't budge.'

We sit in silence for a minute, both ***FUMING***. Parents can just drag you off ***ANYWHERE*** and you have to tag along. There's not much point in being angry so I say what matters most.

'I'll miss you like MAD.'

She nods again and pulls up more grass.

'I wish you could come with us.'

When the bell rings we aren't in a big hurry to get to Geography. In fact, we're the last ones off the playing field and Miss Haliborn is waving to us like a traffic policeman, shouting, *'You are late for afternoon lessons! Will you get a move on?'*

We move slowly, mostly ignoring her, and she eventually marches off to find other kids to shout at. I suppose even Miss Haliborn starts to run out of POISONOUS FUMES by the end of the school year.

Dru sounds like she's had time to think about leaving, like she's already got over the shock.

'We can talk online every day,' she says, suddenly smiling and being her usual optimistic self. 'We can send photos. It's not like we can't keep in touch.'

'And video clips,' I say, liking the idea and pretending to feel optimistic, too. 'We'll nag our parents into getting new technical things so that we can send films of ourselves and where we are, and what we're up to.'

But there's a big OUCH-AND-AN-ACHE underneath my ribs. We're both going to be lonely. We'll both go back to being odd-girls with no friends.

Dru stays late at school for a saxophone lesson, so I make my way home on my own. By the time I get through the door I'm hot, bothered and BROODING like a grumpy goat about her leaving.

Instead of napping on the sofa, like I half-expected, Mum is sitting in the kitchen with Maggie. They're smiling and a bottle of CHAMPAGNE is open on the table – not their usual tea and digestive biscuits.

It shocks me out of my moaning mood.

'What's up?' is all I can think of to say.

Mum sits me down and gives me half an inch of champagne in a glass and passes me an open box of chocolates that I didn't notice when I first came in. Then she goes into a whole BIG LONG explanation of the reason for this mini-party. I don't quite understand all of it, but I understand enough to know that it's BRiLLiANT NEWS.

Mum tells me that when she got poorly and had to leave work to have a rest it was partly because Dad leaving us had made her very sad, but also because of things that had happened at work. She puts her arm around me and offers me another chocolate. I study the little pictures of the different shapes and flavours while she explains to me that Terry Snaul (I still feel sick when I hear his name – but not sick enough to be put off the chocolates) had HARASSED AND BULLIED her. He did this by giving her more work than she could POSSIBLY cope with for weeks and weeks, until she was worn out. He also did 'other things' that she doesn't want to talk about, but I know what she means, of course – she means him behaving like a creep when they went on a date, and then being a bad loser. I want to shout, 'I KNEW it. Didn't I tell you he was BAD NEWS? Didn't I just know he was ALL WRONG the moment I saw his GLOOPY HAIR?!' but I don't shout out, except inside my head, because I'm now chewing a MASSIVE chocolate. Instead, I let her tell me the rest of the story.

Maggie has been sticking up for Mum since she had to leave work. She helped Mum to write letters to people who could do something about Snaulus the Walrus because Mum was too tired and upset to do it herself.

'I could've helped you,' I say. 'Why didn't you ask me?'

'You did help, Coco,' she says, giving me another little squeeze. 'You looked after yourself and me, and Mr Belly. But the letters had to be written by an adult, so I needed Maggie's help, too.'

Mum tells me that she and Maggie had to go

to a lot of 'unpleasant meetings' with people from the office. That must've been really scary for Mum, I realise, when she was afraid to even go out of the house most days. I begin to see that, although Mum was sleepy and useless sometimes, she'd also been doing really brave stuff while I was at school, and Maggie had been her best friend, just like Dru had been mine.

At these 'unpleasant meetings,' Mum explains, she and Maggie said that Terry Snaul had made Mum ill because of his BULLYING. But Terry Snaul said, 'No way! She's just not very good at her job'. Imagine anyone saying that about my mum! **OUTRAGEOUS!** Anyway, they had argued for ages until a judge in a proper court had to sort it out, and he decided that Mum was RIGHT. Terry Snaul is now in BIG trouble and, even better, he is going to have to pay her quite a lot of money. Mum told me that this is called 'compensation' – which means money to make up for the bad things someone has done to you.

'YES! YES! YES!' I shout, because by now I've swallowed the chocolate and I can't hold my shoutiness in any longer. 'MY MUM SQUASHED THE WALRUS MAN!!'

Maggie looks a bit surprised at me, but then she bursts out laughing and I say that I think Mum should have been given a trillion pounds and Snaulus the Walrus should be thrown into a LAKE OF SNOT. I get a bit overexcited then and dance around the kitchen saying,

'Stick that under your wig and dance on it, LARDY BOY!'

which is a good example of times when I forget that I want to be **glamorous** AND *elegant* like Audrey Hepburn and behave like a MAD GIRL.

Mum tries to shush me and says to Maggie, 'I'm really sorry about Cordelia. It's been a difficult time for her, too.'

But Maggie just laughs again and pours more champagne for her and Mum.

When we have all calmed down a bit, especially me, I ask Mum, 'Does that mean that you'll get properly better now?'

'It'll certainly help,' she says. 'I'll have a lot less to worry about and it means I can get someone to help with the cleaning for a little while, and we can decorate the house to make it lovely again.'

My next thought is to tell Dru, which reminds

me, of course, that she won't be here much longer and I suddenly feel DEFLATED, like a popped balloon. All the bounce drains out of me as I tell Mum about Dru leaving. I can see by the way her smile falls away that she knows how important this is to me, and she squeezes me very tightly.

26

'*Excuse me!*'

Ellie Simmons's shouty-posh voice is unmistakable. We are in the corridor and she is tapping me on the shoulder. I spin around to face her. Jen isn't with her. Ellie is hanging out with Gemma Bashir and Liz Tellman these days. Perhaps Jen wasn't posh enough for her.

Who knows?

Who CARES?

Gemma and Liz are just behind Ellie, giggling. Dru is next to me. She pretends to yawn and says, 'Did you hear something, Cordelia?'

'You mean that sound like car brakes screeching?' I ask, meaning Ellie's voice.

Dru nods.

'Yeah.'

I shake my head and shrug.

'Must be outside.'

We both turn to carry on walking down the corridor. Ellie grabs my shoulder and pushes me against the wall. Dru stays beside me.

Ellie yells in my face, 'I said *"Excuse me!"*'

'What d'you want?' I ask, looking her straight in the eye.

She steps back, pulls out a notebook from her pocket and a pen, which she clicks on. I try to walk away again, but Gemma and Liz shove me back. Dru pushes Liz away, but Liz pulls Dru's glasses off and throws them. They go skidding along the corridor. Dru can't do anything without her specs so she has to go after them.

'We're just doing a report for the school magazine called…' Ellie grins nastily and looks at Liz, then at Gemma '…called

"I WANT TO BE A PORN STAR WHEN I LEAVE BECKMERE"

and we thought you might be able to give us some information.'

I don't say anything. I just stare at her. Naked

jokes have been thrown at me ever since THE DEAN EPISODE. She carries on.

'Or there's another article you could probably help us with called

"I HAVE *NO* FRIENDS. AREN'T I PATHETIC?":

Liz and Gemma giggle cattily.

'Or how about…' she moves her face closer.

'"MY DAD: THE LOSER WHO LEFT US":

I still don't say anything. She wants a fight so that she can get me in trouble with Miss Haliborn again, and I'm *NOT* going to give her one. I keep glaring at her. I *CAN'T* believe that I haven't punched her. My teeth are clenched together, like they're holding an explosion in. She waits a few seconds for a reaction. My arm is twitching. I *WANT TO PULL HER HAIR OUT BY THE ROOTS!* But I somehow keep cool on the outside. After a few seconds Ellie sighs, 'Oh, this is *boring*,' and marches off with Liz and Gemma behind her.

Dru comes stumbling back with her glasses.

'Found them! Jeez! I heard that. What a viper! I'm amazed you didn't thump her.'

'So am I,' I say, 'but that doesn't mean I'm going to let her get away with it.'

It's quite easy to steal what I need from the art room. I just slip it out of the supply cupboard and into my bag towards the end of the lesson while Mr Gruber's back is turned. This is BAD and WRONG and SNEAKY. I might have controlled my temper, but I haven't managed to stop doing STUPID things yet.

Dru has to be kept out of my revenge on Ellie Simmons. I don't want her getting into trouble. So I ask to be excused during PE, saying that I need the loo REALLY BADLY.

Miss Haliborn times all our toilet breaks. I have about four and a half minutes.

Of course, I know I'll be found out eventually.

Do I care?

NO.

That girl needs a lesson.

Ellie's things are in a SUPER TIDY pile on her usual part of the bench in the changing rooms. Underneath, her shoes are lined up, side by side. I take the bottle of paint out of my bag and shake the gloopy contents so that they slosh about. A big, squeezable bottle of livid green, mushy pea green,

BOGEY green, SNOT green ready-mixed paint. It's quite heavy, so I tip it up carefully and squirt until both shoes are half full, then I tuck them a little further under the bench so that she won't see them straight away. I throw the rest of the paint bottle into the big rubbish bin in the toilets and cover it with scrunched-up paper towels.

After PE I change VERY quickly and hurry Dru along.

'What's the rush?' she says. 'It's the last lesson.'

'TRUST me,' I whisper sharply. 'We need to leave QUICKLY. I'll explain later.'

On the way to the door I stop in front of Ellie. She's sitting down, buttoning up her crisp, clean blouse. Gemma Bashir nudges her as I approach. Dru stands beside me, probably wondering what on Earth I'm up to.

Ellie curls her top lip when she sees me.

'Did you want something, *nudey girl*?'

'Yes,' I say, pretending to be friendly. 'I've been thinking about your idea. I think I could contribute something to the school magazine, after all.'

She snorts out a nasty little laugh and looks at Liz and Gemma, who also laugh. I nod thoughtfully and stroke my chin.

'I could write an article called

"ELLIE SIMMONS, THE BOGEY QUEEN OF BECKMERE: WE'RE SNOT AMUSED".'

Dru bursts out into a big, loud donkey laugh. I grab her arm and pull her out of the changing rooms before Ellie throttles her.

'That's a good one.' She's still laughing when we are halfway down the corridor. 'I like that. Will you write it?'

At THAT point, when we're almost at the exit, Ellie must've put her shoes on.

'AAAAAAAAAAGGGGGHHHH!'

The scream rings out all over the PE block. Dru looks horrified.

'What did you DO?'

I bite my lip.

'I think I just got expelled.'

27

Dad HAS moved up here! I expected a party, or at least balloons and celebration cake, but it all happened very quietly. Unfortunately, one of the first things he had to do was visit school with Mum to hear about my behaviour from Miss Haliborn.

I was lucky not to get chucked out of school COMPLETELY, or at least suspended for the rest of the year. Instead, I've been put on Report, which means a special journal about my behaviour has to be filled in EVERY DAY by EVERY TEACHER in EVERY LESSON until the end of term. Mum and Dad have to add their comments, too. THANK GOODNESS there are only a couple of weeks left of Year Seven, but it's still a PAIN IN THE REAR.

Ellie got away with just a telling-off for teasing me about what Miss Haliborn called 'unfortunate events' in my school year – meaning the Naked Picture, of course.

Mum and Dad put nice things in my report like 'Cordelia drew costumes from the film *Dr Zhivago* this evening' or 'Cordelia helped make a béchamel sauce tonight'. The things they write make me sound quite interesting and sophisticated.

We have a routine now. Dad comes over to our house every day to help decorate and do some cooking. Our kitchen has spicy smells again and the cupboards are filled with snacks and bulging bags of rice and pasta. If Mum and Dad argue, they don't do it when I'm around, and it's been quite a long time since I last saw Mum looking like she's been crying. I know that I watch Dad very closely and I still get moody with him. One minute I'm cuddly, the next I'm angry, then sulky, then friendly again. Perhaps I'm still worrying and looking for signs that he might disappear. Sometimes this makes me tired and I just wish I could relax about the whole thing. Dru says this will probably take a little while and she keeps reminding me that I MUST stay OPTIMISTIC all the time.

It rains on the DREADED DAY – the day Mum,
Dad and I wave goodbye to Dru and her family.
Their taxi is sagging at the back from all the suitcases.
I hug Dru and we both swear SOLEMNLY that we
will ALWAYS, ALWAYS keep in touch.

Dru's family have given me two special
presents. One is a book on how costumes are
made. It's nearly as big as a tabletop and full of
FANTASTIC pictures. The other is a scrapbook
to keep my own ideas in. It has a hard, green cover
the colour of a champagne bottle and the pages are
heavy and black. I can't stop DROOLING over the
loveliness of these things.

Last hugs now. I give them a BIG bag of sweets
for the journey, which seems a very small present
compared to theirs and I'm a bit embarrassed.
But I did give Dru my favourite picture of Audrey
Hepburn, which I know she loves.

There are lots of kisses being blown, and
waving, and Dru leans out of the taxi window
shouting, 'EVERYTHING'S GOING TO BE
FINE, CORDELIA!'

So I run after them as their taxi pulls away.

Meanwhile, Jess is tugging at the back of Dru's jeans to get her inside the car. 'I KNOW, I'M AN OPTIMIST NOW!' I yell.

Then the taxi turns the corner and she's gone. I'm on my own, with my parents still not quite together again and I'm not 100% sure that they ever will be.

There have to be SOME tear-jerkingly romantic reunions in real life. SURELY things like that don't JUST happen in films. People who make films must get their ideas from somewhere. I imagine Mum and Dad standing in the rain like at the end of *Breakfast at Tiffany's* (and lots of other films), hugging our cat and each other, and me driving the taxi that is waiting to whisk them off into a happy ending.

Hmmm. Yes, I think I'd be driving.

But, I know, I know. Real life is never QUITE like films.

28

Dru and I start chatting online as soon as she's back in Seattle. There's only one week to go before the end of term here but the schools in America have already finished for the summer so lucky old Dru is already FREE. I'm SO jealous! She sends AMAZING photos of Seattle. I have VOWED to go there one day. Her messages are clever and funny and they REALLY help me to survive because all I can see ahead is a long stretch of summer holiday with Mum and Dad NOT QUITE TOGETHER, followed by another year at Beckmere where all the teachers have already told me they'll be keeping an eye on me. I'm writing to Dru now to get advice on my latest disasters.

★ **Cordelia** to Dru

Dru, HELP!

How will I survive?

Mr Gruber is leaving next year!

Art classes are the **ONLY** thing keeping me **SANE**. I told him I might have to **SLASH** his tyres and he laughed, but that's what I **FEEL** like doing. How could he **ABANDON** me?

And Mr Grimpson is moving to a hut in the woods to write a novel. English won't even be **MILDLY INTERESTING** without his ridiculous clothes to laugh at.

I'll probably end up having Miss Haliborn for **EVERYTHING** and she still **HATES** me.

EVERYONE is **ABANDONING** me to some **TERRIBLE FATE**.

DOUBLE HELP!!

C xxx

P.S. We're going to the seaside next week, which is a major breakthrough because, not long ago, Dad said he didn't think Mum would 'entertain the idea' of a holiday together. How can I leave them alone enough for it to be romantic?

Her reply comes quickly.

★ **Dru** to Cordelia

Cordelia...**STOP PANICKING!**

YOU ARE SUCH A `'DRASTIC DRAWERS'`
SOMETIMES

NOTE THESE POINTS:

1. You might get an **EVEN BETTER** art
   teacher! Allow that possibility to
   SEEP into your brain.

2. I think a hut in the woods is the
   best place for Mr Grimpson. It may
   be good therapy for his obsession
   with grammar.

3. Miss Haliborn probably isn't
   qualified to teach **ANYTHING** except
   PE so don't worry.

4. About the holiday. My advice is as
   follows:

a) Tag along with another family, even
   if they do boring stuff. That way
   your parents will be **FORCED** to
   spend long periods of time walking

along the beach together.

b) Keep saying, 'I'm just going to look in this shop; you two wait for me on a bench.' This way they **HAVE** to spend ages sitting on benches, chatting.

c) Eat a big lunch then announce, just before dinner, that you don't have room for **ANOTHER CRUMB**. Tell them they should **GO AHEAD** and you'll be **PERFECTLY HAPPY** on your own with the television while they're at the restaurant. That way they will **HAVE** to spend time eating and talking together.

Hope these help. Send progress report.

Dru XX

So the school year has finally ended and here we are by the sea. I'm doing my best to follow Dru's guidelines, but the only family available to 'tag along with' are SO brainy and *posh* that I don't think I can face spending a second or third afternoon with them. It's not that they're unfriendly – I just don't understand what they're talking about sometimes and they don't joke around very much. They're obsessed with identifying every living thing they see and finding its Latin name in their collection of dictionaries and encyclopaedias. When they find it they all shout

TRA-LA-LA...BING! FANTASTICO!

and laugh like gurgling drains. They give each other Latin nicknames and talk about opera (which leaves me out as I've never seen one). They don't even mention the costumes! Then they all go back to their cottage in the evening and play violins together. Not that there's anything wrong with violins, but I can't even play a tune on the recorder so I can't join in AT ALL. They probably think I'm a COMPLETE IGNORAMUS.

I'm doing better with the shop-browsing idea. Mum and Dad have waited patiently together on several benches while I nosed around in the shops pretending to be interested in HIDEOUS tourist souvenirs. Can someone please explain to me why this super-ugly junk that no one wants is sold AT ALL and why a souvenir of the English seaside would have 'Made in China' stamped on it?

Much more importantly, I've managed to NOT have dinner with Mum and Dad on TWO occasions, which has left me STARVING because even a huge lunch doesn't last long in all this fresh sea air. Mum and Dad have probably guessed what I'm up to, but that hasn't stopped them from going along with it, which MUST mean that they WANT to be alone together.

All week, Mum and I have shared the twin bedroom in the little cottage we're renting, and Dad has slept on the sofa bed in the tiny living room. It's a bit weird. Mums and dads usually share, don't they, unless one of them snores like a warthog? But the business of 'sleeping arrangements' is probably not something I should try and influence, being twelve and not REALLY knowing all that much about sex. Besides! These are my PARENTS, for goodness' sake! A girl could damage her mind thinking about such things.

I'm quite happy just setting up a 'potentially romantic' situation.

They are DEFINITELY more relaxed with each other and last night, when they let me stay behind and watch television for the SECOND time. I pretended to be asleep on the sofa when they came back, hoping that Dad might leave me there and end up in my bed.

But that trick didn't work.

He woke me up very gently and moved me

back into the twin room. But I heard Mum giggle when they came back to the cottage, like they'd had a really good time and might even be getting a bit soppy and kissy. So that was

TRA-LA-LA...BING! FANTASTICO!

29

We've only been back from the holiday for a couple of days but Granny Twigg has just appeared on the doorstep without any warning. Straight away, she starts an ALMIGHTY ROW, mostly with Dad, but Mum is there, too, trying to calm it all down, being MUCH nicer to Granny Twigg than she deserves. GT doesn't even ask if I'm at home or if I'm well. I listen from the stairs but I can't quite hear everything they say. I don't particularly want to see Granny Twigg so I stay where I am, and then dart back upstairs as soon as her taxi drives off and get on the computer to tell Dru.

★ **Cordelia** to Dru

Dru – **HELP!**

You won't believe the **WINDOW-RATTLING ROW** that's just been going on here. I'm not sure what it was all about.

Granny Twigg arrived out of the blue (I've told you about my **VENOMOUS GRANNY**, haven't I?)

This is what I earwigged:

MUM: We haven't discussed it as a family yet.

GRANNY TWIGG: And will I be included in these 'family discussions'?

(Nose screwed up, like she's just smelled poo. Not that I saw her, but I can imagine.)

DAD: No, you won't be. It's not really anything to do with you, is it? This is a decision for us and Cordelia.

GT: She was **MY** sister.

DAD: And you never had a good word to say about her, or *to* her.

MUM: It's all right, John (that's Dad's name). Why don't you take Coco to the shop? I need some more milk. Mum, what about a cup of tea? Let's all calm down a bit, eh?

GT: I'll never visit you if you move there.

DAD: All the more reason to go.

MUM: John! That's not necessary. Mum? Cup of tea? John? Milk, please.

GT: Don't bother with any tea. I'm not stopping. I know where I stand.

DAD: Good.

GT: Your opinion of me is clear enough.

MUM: Just stay for a cuppa, Mum.

GT: Don't try and win me round with cups of tea. No doubt you'll be offering chocolate biscuits, too. You were always a sly one. The **LORD KNOWS** what I did to deserve a daughter like you, a daughter who'd diddle me out of my own inheritance.

DAD: That's it! Enough! Either you apologise to Ellen (that's Mum) or you leave immediately. (I could hear Mum crying now.)

GT: You picked a fine **NOBODY** to marry, you did, my girl.

You're both as bad. In this together, I see.

Then Dad put Granny Twigg's big suitcase outside the front door and called a taxi, and she was gone in less than ten minutes because Dad called Marlon's Cabs round the corner and they're really quick.

Will write again as soon as I find out more.

Miss you.

Cordelia xx

I put *Brief Encounter* on and TRY to stay upstairs watching it until the STEAM has gone out of whatever is happening with Mum and Dad. But it doesn't work. I'm just too nosey and I have to give up on the film, even though I was just getting a really good drawing of how the man's hanky sticks out of his top pocket in the scene where he falls in love at first sight. These details are CRUCIAL on a good costume. Anyway, it's no good, I can't concentrate because my brain is VERY DISTRACTED by trying to work out what the row was all about, so I creep downstairs and past the kitchen door and outside to where Mr Belly is wriggling on our tiny lawn like he's still a kitten. I'm just tickling him with a long piece of grass when Dad calls, 'Coco. Come in for a minute, please.'

Dad was decorating the hall when Granny Twigg INVADED. His blue overalls are covered in Daffodil Yellow paint splatters.

I pretend to be calm and only a little bit interested. 'What is it?'

He waves me inside and we sit down with Mum at the kitchen table. She's shuffling through a fat pile of papers that have come out of a brown envelope. I saw the postman deliver this a couple of days ago. Mum looks business-like, but she and Dad are both a bit fidgety, like they are about to announce something MASSIVE and aren't sure how I'm going to take it. I'm not sure, either.

It turns out to be about as surprising as anything could POSSIBLY be.

'Well. What? WHAT!?' I say, sounding like a proper little brat and wishing I'd said it differently, but this is suddenly making me SO tense and worried. 'Sorry,' I say, 'but I'm not DEAF, I heard most of that row, and I feel like you're not TELLING ME what's going on. I HATE THAT.'

Mum raises her hand very slightly to show that I should 'just hang on a minute and stop flying off the handle'. She says, 'Do you remember Auntie Deirdre?'

'Lah-di-dah Deirdre? Granny Twigg's sister?'

'Yes,' says Mum. 'Well, you remember that she died last year?'

'Yes.'

I was at the funeral. OF COURSE I remember. I wish Mum would spit out whatever she's going to say. I try to breathe deeply and not be a SOUR FACE.

'Well,' says Mum, 'it took a very long time to sort out her money after she died, but I have just heard that she's left us a property in her will.'

'Like a house?'

'Yes. Well, more than a house – a pub with a barn and a cottage and a bit of land.'

'Are we moving?'

I WISH they'd just break it to me.

'We have to talk about that,' says Dad. 'We won't make any decisions unless you're happy with them.'

'Is that why Granny was here?'

Mum and Dad look at each other, like they are checking that they both think it's OK to tell me more. Then they look back to me, and Mum says, 'Yes. Granny is a bit upset that the property wasn't left to her. That's why it took so long to sort out. We told her on the phone last week that she'll always be very welcome to stay there, if we decide to move. But she doesn't seem happy with that. She thinks it should be hers.'

Dad is looking down at the floor. I bet it wasn't HIM who told Granny Twigg she could visit whenever she likes. Mum sees me looking at Dad and shuffles, like she's uncomfortable in her seat. She gives a little cough to get Dad's attention, and then she carries on.

'I think Granny feels a bit pushed out, a bit forgotten.'

'Well, she shouldn't have been HORRID to Auntie Deirdre, then, should she?' I say.

Mum goes a bit pink because she knows I am just telling the truth, but she doesn't like to think that her mum is a GRIZZLY OLD WITCH.

'It serves Granny Twigg right,' I add.

'I don't think she likes the idea of your dad having a share of it,' says Mum. 'She and Dad have never really got along.'

My mouth drops open slightly. Mum is SO soft.

'She doesn't get along with ANYONE,' I blurt out. 'You're too kind to her. She needs a good telling-off, I think. If I was as rude to people as she is you'd never give me pocket money EVER again and I'd be grounded FOR EVER. Just because people get old doesn't mean we should let them treat us like DOG POO, does it?'

Dad is looking down again. He's pretending to wipe the corners of his mouth with his fingers, but

I can tell he's trying not to laugh. Mum nudges him under the table and he stops and puts on a serious face. Mum has more to say.

'You're quite right, Coco. But daughters do put up with some odd behaviour from their mothers, don't they?' She smiles. 'Look at what you put up with from me recently.'

'But that's different. You're nice. She's POISONOUS.'

Dad's head goes down again. Mum nudges him again. This time I think she's trying to tell him that it's his turn to say something, and he does.

'Well, anyway. She's a bit upset with us just now, but I think she'll come around once she sees how nice we make the place… If we go… If you like it and want to move there.'

'What's it like?' I ask.

Dad sits up and gets enthusiastic, so I can tell he REALLY wants me to like the idea.

'Mum and I have had a look at the place – but we won't make any decisions without you because it would mean a change of school – but we think the pub would make a great restaurant and the big barn at the back could become a little cinema.'

Change of school? GREAT, I thought. No

more Miss Haliborn.

Restaurant? ALSO GREAT.

Cinema? TRA-LA-LA…BING! FANTASTICO!!

'Of course, there's quite a lot of work to be done on it,' Mum says, and she lays some photos out on the table and turns them around so that I can see. She's right about the work. There's a hole in the roof and the windows are boarded up. It doesn't look like much and it DEFINITELY looks like it's in the middle of nowhere. I'd hoped it would be near Paris or Rome or London or somewhere else big and glamorous.

'Are there trains?' I ask.

Dad nods.

'The station is in the next village. We can be in London in a couple of hours.'

'Will I have a nice room?'

'Very nice, and very big,' Mum chips in. 'As soon as we get the roof fixed. But you don't have to decide now, Coco. We can drive out tomorrow and have a look.'

But I don't think I need to. I don't care about holes in the roof. I just need to know one thing for certain.

'Will it DEFINITELY be all three of us?'

Mum looks at Dad. I think she's holding her breath as he explains.

'Mum and I will always be very good friends,' he begins.

I don't like the sound of this. Friends isn't like being married or living together, is it? I'm also holding my breath now. The room is very still because only Dad seems to be breathing and talking. I can feel myself getting hot.

'We want to set up this new business together… the restaurant and the cinema. We want to help each other with that and we both want to see you every day.'

I'm still not breathing.

'But Mum isn't ready to have me living with her again and I have to respect that.'

I look at Mum. She's as still as a statue.

'What we thought might be best to start with is to have you and Mum stay in the little cottage attached to the pub while I have a caravan in the big field at the back. That way we can still have dinner together every day and live close by. What d'you think?'

A caravan in a field doesn't sound very nice to me. I have to breathe out so I can speak.

'How long will you be living there for?'

'Just until the building work is done,' says Dad. 'Then you and Mum will have a nice big flat above the restaurant and I'll have the little cottage.'

'So you're not going to live together like before?'

'Not at the moment, Coco.'

All I can say is, 'I need to think.'

I pick Mr Belly up and go back outside to the tiny lawn. I sit down cross-legged and stroke his big ginger head while I close my eyes and try to picture what it would really be like. It's not exactly what I wanted. Life wouldn't be like it was before Dad went away. But I imagine Mum selling tickets for the cinema and Dad rustling up fantastic food in a lovely kitchen for lots of happy customers. I remember that this is their 'vision' just like mine is to be the greatest costume designer in the history of cinema. This is what they both want to do most, and if they do that, they'll both be happy, won't they? And if they're both happy, they might fall in love with each other again. It's not the ending I expected, but we're all there, no one is missing, and we're all doing what makes us happy.

I go back inside, leaving Mr Belly on the grass. Mum and Dad are still at the table. They look up when I come in.

I just nod and say, 'OK, let's do it. Let's go and live there.'

Mum and Dad give a big sigh at the same time. Then Dad shouts, 'Champagne!'

Dad runs to the shop to get a bottle specially – I get my usual half-inch of champagne in a tumbler. We're soon sitting around the kitchen table swapping ideas for the new restaurant and cinema. I ask Dad, 'If I'd said no, what would you have done?'

'Oh, that's easy.'

He sips his champagne to make me wait for the answer.

'We'd have sent you to live with Granny Twigg.'

Mum and Dad look at my HORRIFIED face. It's the first time in ages that I've seen them both burst out laughing at the same time.

'JOKE!' they shout.

Of course, I have to contact Dru before bed and explain the WHOLE THING. I'm missing her so much right now, when everything is suddenly changing again. She replies pretty quickly.

★ **Dru** to Cordelia

Cordelia - Hi!

WHOOPS of JOY!!

I'm **SO** pleased for you and your
mom and dad. It sounds like a good
arrangement for now.

Don't worry about being 'in the
sticks'. That's why transport and the
internet were invented, right?

The plan has been a **TOTAL SUCCESS**.
And I reckon you deserve **BONUS
POINTS** for getting a new home *and*
school *and* your parents starting a
new business.

We're off to the beach for a couple
of weeks!

YIPPEE!!

Will write as soon as I find an
internet café.

Will send postcard, too.

Jess says 'hi'.

Love Dru xx

30

This morning is our big move. I've just supervised my film collection being put into the removal van and am running to the shop to see if the latest copy of *Stars and Screen* has come in. I'll need some lemon sherbets for the journey as well – two hours into deepest nowhere. I might never see another lemon sherbet or a copy of *Stars and Screen* again! I hope Mum and Dad fully appreciate the sacrifices I'm making for this adventure.

Our house is fresh and clean now and smells of new paint and furniture polish. There are daisy-print curtains in the kitchen and warm, green velvet ones in the living room. The little garden is trimmed and neat. We're renting it to a woman who used to live near Drusilla's family in Seattle. She works for the same company as Dru's dad.

I'm reaching for *Stars and Screen* from the shelf in the corner shop when Jen walks in. She's on her own, which is unusual for her. I swallow hard and decide to be brave. After all, I might never see her again.

'Hi,' I say.

She doesn't reply straight away and I think to myself, Oh well, the usual ICICLE TREATMENT. At least I tried. But then I think, What have I got to lose? So I try again.

'I'm moving today,' I say.

Jen looks at me then, but doesn't say, 'Hi, Cordelia.' She just asks, 'Where to?'

I tell her about the restaurant and the cinema, but leave out the bit about the holes in the roof and Dad living in a caravan – both DEEPLY UNGLAMOROUS.

Jen just says, 'Oh.'

'I'm sorry we fell out,' I say.

Jen shrugs. 'Doesn't matter now.'

'I'm sorry I said horrid things to you. I was unhappy…you know…about Dad.'

Jen nods. 'I'm glad he came back.'

'Thanks.'

There's a little pause, then Jen adds, 'Good luck. I hope your new school's nice.' Which probably was quite hard for her to say. Then she takes a deep breath and starts to tell me about Dean Frampton.

'His dad is sending him off to a boy's boarding school where he'll have to do cross-country runs every morning and have cold showers and where there are no girls for a hundred miles.'

We both laugh a little bit, but not for long, not like we're best friends again or anything. I'm a bit stuck for something else to say, and I think Jen feels like the conversation has just about run out, too, so I think I should go. I pay for the magazine and lemon sherbets and just say, 'Bye, Jen. Have a good summer.'

She gives a little wave. 'Yeah, have fun.'

And I walk home thinking, OK, it wasn't a big LET'S BE FRIENDS AGAIN scene, but it was enough. Any bad feelings between us have gone just with that tiny conversation. Sometimes just a few words can change everything. Jen and I are very different now, but we don't need to waste energy on hating each other.

297

Twenty minutes later and I'm strapped into the back seat of our car, sucking lemon sherbets and reading about a big film that has won an Oscar for the costume designs. Mr Belly is in his carrying basket next to me and Mum and Dad are arguing about what music to put on. Both of them have TERRIBLE TASTE, but I'll just ENDURE whatever noise they agree on because the sound of them talking like normal parents is quite relaxing.

Mum is driving for the first time in months so Dad looks a bit worried and keeps reminding her to indicate or speed up or slow down. I'll just listen and crunch my lemon sherbets and read my magazine. Now that my parents are on their way to being sorted out I can concentrate on becoming **the** *⋆* **GREATEST** *⋆* **costume designer in the history of cinema**. So, if you'll excuse me, I must read this article:

The heroine gets her first kiss in a long dress made of red silk. The high neckline is encrusted with freshwater pearls. The shoes were handmade for the actress in satin...

So glamorous!

Acknowledgements

A **BIG, FAT, JUICY THANK YOU** to all the people who made it possible for me to share Cordelia with you. Here are a few of them:

My parents, for launching me into the world in the first place. The amazing Saras and all the team at Undiscovered Voices, who work very, very, very hard indeed. Alice Williams at David Higham Associates and Catherine Coe at Orchard for loving Cordelia. Everyone else at Orchard for their fabulous creative input. David Roberts for his scrumptious artwork. Jane, Kevin, Beth, Joe and Catherine, the kindest and brainiest family in the universe, for their friendship and support through life's ups and downs over many years. Robert, for not letting me wimp out at any point, and for buying lots of chocolate. And Ewan, who is wise and strong and very patient with his strange mother.

A Q&A with **CLAIRE O'BRIEN**,
author of

CORDELIA CODD
Not Just the Blues

Cordelia has always dreamed of being a costume designer. Did you always dream of being a writer?

I didn't start writing my own stories until I was in my twenties, but from a very young age I liked writing by hand with a pencil, fountain pen or on my dad's old typewriter. I spent hours copying text out of encyclopaedias (I was a strange child). I think I enjoyed the peace and quiet and concentration. But my own stories came much later.

*What do you do to make yourself feel better when you have **FURIOUS RED FEELINGS**?*

I try not to say anything while I'm still cross. Going for a long bike ride helps – it gives me thinking space and calms me down.

Is Breakfast at Tiffany's *one of your favourite films, like Cordelia?*

It's certainly one of my favourites, but there are so many great films out there that it's nearly impossible to have an absolute favourite. At the moment I think my top choices would be:

- For glamorous costumes: *Pandora and the Flying Dutchman* (1951)
- For tear-jerking loveliness and great dancing: *Billy Elliot* (2000)
- For giggles: The original St. Trinian's films, especially *The Belles of St. Trininan's* (1954)
- For laughter and romance and something new: *The Artist* (2011)

Do Cordelia's mum and dad get back together at the end?

I'm not saying. Do you think they should?
Is getting back together always the best thing?

Are you similar to any of the characters in the book, like Cordelia or Dru?

I think Cordelia and Dru are both a bit brainier than I was at their age, especially Dru. I did like art lessons, like Cordelia, but, unlike Cordelia, I didn't have a clue what I wanted to do when I grew up.

Cordelia finds school really stressful until she becomes friends with Dru. Did you like school?

I liked having friends to hang out with, but the discipline wasn't very good at my school so there was a lot of bullying. That part could have been better.

How long did it take to write Not Just the Blues*?*

AGES. The first draft took about nine months. At that time no one wanted to publish it so I put it in a drawer for about TWO YEARS. When I took it out I spent another six months making changes, then more changes, before I sent it to anyone. By the time Orchard Books spotted it and wanted to publish it, I had changed it at least five times. Then I had to make some more changes before it was completely ready. You have to be very patient and hard working to be an author.

Are you happy with your writing when you've finished or do you always want to change things?

There is always something that you could improve,

but eventually you have to LET GO and move on to the next story.

Do you have lots of ideas for more books?

About a zillion. I hope I live to be very, very old so that I have time to write them all.

What are your favourite books?

I like lots of different books for different reasons. A few are:

- *Tom's Midnight Garden* by Philippa Pearce – the first book that I just couldn't put down
- *Coram Boy* by Jamila Gavin – scary and beautiful and really well written
- *Krindlekrax* by Philip Ridley – brilliantly funny and sad at the same time
- *Private Peaceful* by Michael Morpurgo – beautifully written, heart-breakingly tragic and shows us why we should never go to war

Do you have any advice for anyone wanting to be an author?

Only become an author if there is absolutely nothing else that will make you happy. It is a very tough job. But if you really do want to do it, try to read a lot, keep a notebook with you all the time and don't let anyone persuade you to change your mind.

What are the best and worst parts about being an author?

The worst part is that until you are published everyone thinks you are just a dreamer who should go and get a proper job – so you have to believe in yourself. The best part is that you send stories out into the world that no one else could have written. You create something unique and hopefully make lots of people smile.

Ask Claire a question of your own!
Visit her website at
www.claireobrien.co.uk